Christopher Best

THE OLD MEN AND THE PUB

Limited Special Edition. No. 24 of 25 Paperbacks

Christopher Best spent most of his working life in the city. Beginning in insurance at age fifteen, he was a naïve Eastender who had never seen a bowler hat in the flesh until his first day at work. By the end of his career, he was working for financial magazines, editing and writing them. On early retirement, he took to writing fiction. His first novel was written for children but with enough meat in it to engage adults – 'kidult' work.

This book is dedicated to those friends and workmates whose shared experience it fondly remembers and records.

Christopher Best

THE OLD MEN AND THE PUB

AUSTIN MACAULEY PUBLISHERS™

LONDON • CAMBRIDGE • NEW YORK • SHARJAH

A CIP catalogue record for this title is available from the British Library.

ISBN 9781528934299 (Paperback)
ISBN 9781528934305 (Hardback)
ISBN 9781528967822 (ePub e-book)

www.austinmacauley.com

First Published (2019)
Austin Macauley Publishers Ltd
25 Canada Square
Canary Wharf
London
E14 5LQ

I owe it to my wife, Edda, for uncomplainingly reading and correcting my original effort and its numerous rewrites, and for her many suggestions for improving the writing and storyline – most of which were taken on board.

Thanks also to Rob and Patricia Davies for reading chapters in the manuscript as they emerged, and for continually reassuring me, enthusiastically, that it was worth my plodding on, a matter about which I frequently had doubts.

Chapter 1

Five men mature enough to be philosophical at hearing themselves described as old geezers were making their way to a lunchtime appointment. It was a get-together at a pub; at least a few pints, probably more, and a bite to eat. But unbeknown to them each had another, and fateful appointment, some five or six hours later in the day. Determinists would argue that both appointments had been on the cards, scheduled and inescapable, since the beginning of time.

The old men's get-together today was not a meeting of any special significance in itself. They all knew that very well; it was a repeat of many similar 'socials' held regularly (usually never at a greater interval than two or three months) over the past five decades of their lives. But each of them would have been disappointed and even slightly shamefaced – it is no exaggeration to say shamefaced – if unable, and for whatever reason short of serious illness, to make it: yet again.

These get-togethers had become, as indicated, a habit continued across the decades…for so long indeed that they acquired the status of obligation, as habits will when they do not simply fade away.

It was a cold November morning in London, nearly mid-day, and a slight drizzle in the air. One of the old geezers, a tall round-faced bespectacled man in his early seventies – and looking every year of it, incidentally – scant of hair, wearing a shabby raincoat, was walking rapidly along the pavement southwards under Holborn Viaduct. His blank and fixed look might have conveyed, if anyone were interested in reading it – but he was old, so most would not have been – that he was bent upon his destination. He had the zombie look of office workers who every day stream across London Bridge to their tryst with insurance or banking. This old man was going somewhere else, however. He had a slight limp, but it did not slow him down.

Catching sight of the plate glass window of a new vape shop down a side turning, the man, Jim Anderton, recalled having passed by only a few weeks ago when it had still been a bookstore. He estimated that Jenkin's Book Shop had plied its civilising trade on the same site for several decades, at least. *Jesus,* he thought. Easily irritated, he gave the vape shop the deeply offended look which he also used on nail bars and mobile phone shops: new shops in general. But he continued his brisk pace down Farringdon Street towards Ludgate Circus, briskly despite his limp. One more sign of everything going to the dogs was neither here nor there given the general collapse on all fronts, and certainly no reason for him to slow his pace or allow his purpose to be blunted. If anything, it whetted his purpose.

Another fifty yards and he could see, still a little farther off and on the other side of the road, the suspended sign swinging in the wind advertising the Slug and Lettuce, the pub he was headed for. A shudder racked him, whether caused by irritation at some change in the world about him, or by physical pain, or by the cold wind, no observer of Jim could have judged with anything like certainty.

Jim's shudder was caused not by the biting November wind, nor, as we shall see, by the left knee that was scheduled for replacement in six months' time according to the consultant. Cold wind and knee pain he could cope with stoically. *Bloody six years, more likely, not six months, the way the No Health Service is going,* Jim thought to himself bitterly, suddenly remembering his appointment when his knee gave him a twinge. *Down the tubes it's going…* Jim began to commune testily with his inner self, forgetting for the moment the cause of his seemingly involuntary shudder.

'Make economies, the government says, and now the old NHS has finally twigged – the gits behind the desks have anyway: keep the buggers on the hop. That's their mantra now: keep 'em waiting.' (By this time, Jim was not merely moving his lips in sync with his thoughts, he was speaking them out loud – a disconcerting experience for passers-by, who in the main dealt with it by giving him wide passage.)

'Then the suckers'll kick the bucket and disappear up the crematorium chimney in good time,' Jim laughed. 'In good time for all their appointments to be transferred to worthier causes: gender reassignments, for instance. That'll certainly shorten the waiting lists for the NHS. Or should I say...N *H*aitch S, as they now pronounce it? I should cocoa.

'Yep, I can just see it,' Jim concluded, much to his own satisfaction: 'the N Haitch S's own version of the bucket list. A register of all the old-uns calculated to kick it long before their appointment with surgery – the appointment an entirely notional idea in the first place anyway, a moveable feast if ever there was one.'

Jim's shudder, to come back to that, was a response he could not control – actually did not want to because he got a peculiar masochistic satisfaction from it. It happened – Jim brought it on, to be more accurate – whenever he came across a renamed pub, especially one he had known under its old name. (Given Jim's nature, there were many other aspects of modern life that caused him to shudder irritably, on demand as it were.) Even if he had not previously been to a pub, he still knew whether its name had changed. 'How could you fail to,' he would tell people; 'most pubs have been around for ages, so if the name sounds new, it can't be the pub's original one. Enough said.'

'Who is going to call a pub The Nelson, The Duke of Windsor, The Lamb and Flag, The King's Head, The Nell Gwynne, The Waterman's Arms, The Alma, The Ticket Porter, The Rifleman's Arms, The Steam Packet – nowadays? On the other hand, nobody sixty years ago, in their right mind or even completely out of it, would've dreamt of calling a pub The Slug and Fucking Lettuce. Or even The Slug and Lettuce.'

Jim could have given you a well-honed tirade on the inanity of pub-naming today. He had thought it through, imagined to himself the young executive with slimline briefcase and Mondeo who'd worked through the spreadsheets to discover what today's pub demographic expected its drinking hole to be called. 'The bleedin' Slug and Lettuce.' But today's semi private rehearsal of the tirade was brought short by Jim's arrival at the – what *used* to be The Rifleman.

Jim was to meet four of his old mates for what they still laughably called a booze-up; he knew that if they got through three or four pints before somebody suggested eating something it would be a bloody marvel. *Gone are the old days,* he thought, smiling at the recollection, *when we could get plastered and still wake up next day with nothing worse than a mild hangover, instantly curable with a fry-up, and then do the same the next night.*

Andy Patton had got to the pub a bit earlier than Jim and secured one-half of a wide mock alcove which had banquette seating all around. The few chairs on the open sides of the table which Andy had secured – the table being rectangular and surfaced with some indeterminate composite – were also upholstered to match the banquette. The upholstering is mentioned only as another feature likely to irritate Jim. Proper pubs had wooden tables and wooden seats, so that a bit of spillage was neither here nor there; usually all over the place in fact.

Jim's invariable sensation on passing through the door of a pub was a sharp pang, a constriction in the chest caused by disappointment, disbelief, and a strong sense of unfairness – the sort of pang common on hearing of the death of your nearest and dearest. Only it was not a bereavement, not in the conventional sense, that caused Jim's pang.

Yet again, as Jim entered the Slug and Lettuce, there was no warm, inviting and enveloping smell of beer, wafting from the beer-impregnated walls and floorings and furniture – promise of simple and innocent, and totally satisfying pleasure to come. That was what caused the pang. It worked like this: the very absence of the longed-for aroma, which for so many years since his youth was associated in Jim's mind with entering a pub, triggered Jim's olfactory memory whenever he now crossed the threshold. For a moment, the old smell would be in his nostrils again – in his imagination. Then the moment gone, the pang of disappointment...

Of course, *no* pubs now welcomed patrons ("punters" nowadays no doubt) with the smell of yesteryear that Jim sought; they hadn't for decades.

But for Jim, passing through the door of a pub acted on him in the way a nibble of madeleine did on Proust: it brought back a host of memories. First came the aforementioned olfactory memory; then, after the pang of disappointment, came all the memories of how things once were in the golden age. Lastly, of course, and pretty quickly, there came an awareness of the fall from grace. It felt like the loss of an empire – and it was in a way: Jim's empire of youth. Not much of an empire, he knew: geographically stretching not more than a few hundred yards in any direction from its centre, approximately the Lamb in Leadenhall Market.

And there was also the empire of the mind, Jim's mind, that was long gone; its colonies had comprised county cricket at its best, when Surrey won the championship seven years' running in the fifties; pubs as they used to be, as alluded to; holidays at the seaside in England – reassuringly always the same; Lyons and the ABC never more than a short walk away in any town centre, where rosy-faced women called you "ducks" and didn't say "no worries" when you asked for a tea or insist you "have a nice day"; libraries with books in them, and you wouldn't find the Memoirs of Derek Nimmo under "Literature"; the extended family of aunts, uncles and cousins; secure jobs and careers for life; an England that still had a smattering of self-confidence and where you were allowed to be proud of its history – some small part of its history, at least.

A terrible wind of change had blown it all away. Gone and forgotten were all the great ones who trod the earth in Jim's youth, peerless men (of course they *were* men) – Len Hutton, Rocky Marciano, Stanley Matthews, Churchill, of course, Max Miller, Charles Trenet, John Ford...

'Jim, over here, old boy.'

An elderly man, the aforementioned Andy Patton as it happens, who was under medium height, pock-marked and fleshy, snub-nosed, moist, lethargic and generally unhealthy-looking, but nevertheless sturdy in frame with a reasonable amount of wiry dark hair left – this elderly man, whom Jim could see at a glance wasn't Lady Diana, shouted his greeting while doing a pointless semaphore with his arms and simultaneously attempting the impossible: to get into a standing position starting from where he was – hemmed in behind an immovable table.

If you had reason to drop a plumb line from the inside edge of the table's top, it would have hit the banquettes. So once you were in situ, the most you could do if you wanted to get up for a pee or to greet someone, or bugger off home, was a half sitting, half standing job followed by a side-shuffle to freedom. And if you went at it too fast, you would likely have a dent in your thighs for a week or two. For reasons privy to the pub trade the table was screwed to the floor. Jim entertained the idea that perhaps there were patrons who'd steal free-standing tables now there weren't any ashtrays to swipe.

'Christ, am I supposed to get my belly behind that?' Jim said, giving a cursory nod of recognition to his friend of fifty years' standing. 'I think I'll sit this side on one of these here Queen Anne things.'

'George'll be a bit late,' Andy informed Jim, 'central lines up the creek – he sent a text about five minutes ago. How's your knee by the way? I got you that,' he said, pointing to a pint of bitter. 'It's McMullen's, they don't do your usual here.'

'It's fine, thanks,' and Jim downed about a third of it to show no hard feelings.

'Besides, after the first few, they all taste the same, don't they?' he said.

Jim was now sufficiently relaxed – the anticipation of the beer's effect was enough – to take off his raincoat and chuck it on the next seat, and sigh as after a task satisfactorily completed.

'That's better – beginning to feel almost human again.'

'Anything happened since the last beano?' Andy asked.

'No, but the knee's a bit more of a bugger – especially at night.' After a minute's silence, it occurred to Jim that some manifestation of interest in what happens to others was called for. He did care about his friends – deep down – but it was a chore going through the formalities, and it was all too easy to err in the other direction: show too much emotion and embarrass everyone. Jim and his friends knew by instinct that for men of their generation and age repression was the tried and tested technique for coping with feelings.

'And you?'

'Yeah, fine. That trip Jane and me had in southern Italy last month – I definitely wouldn't recommend it. Hours in coaches every day through the flattest landscape you've ever seen, and churches by the dozen done out like fairground rides – plaster in every colour of the rainbow, hideous religious daubs, church bling; people videoing and photographing all the crap. If it's beauty you're looking for, there's more on Blackpool Pier. Jane didn't like it when I said that.'

'Know what you mean, Andy.' Jim said, nodding sagely.

'And the hot weather killed my feet. Done anything since the last beano? Oh, I asked that already, didn't I?'

'Not really,' Jim answered. 'Gardening, rereading Dickens – Bleak House at present... Went to one of those live opera broadcasts at the local cinema last week, with Maureen, of course. Gotterdammerung from the Met – not a bundle of laughs but some great stuff in it. I think I'd like to kick off, when the time comes, which I trust won't be too long, like Brunhilda. You know the story?' Andy obviously didn't, so Jim paraphrased: 'At the end the whole world's ablaze and she just gets on her horse and gallops into the worst bit singing her head off. And Bob's your uncle. Trouble with these live opera broadcasts, though, is that the average age of the audience is always at least ninety; I exaggerate – but not much.

'Sitting in on one of those things makes you realise that becoming old is also, in effect, joining a completely different bloody species: the youngsters on the doors look at you with blank incomprehension. I kid you not, old friend – they can't, they simply can't imagine how you can get anything out of it. They hear it, I s'pose, like your cat hears it. Ah, well – God moves in mysterious ways and all that.'

They both looked into the middle distance, as if recalling significant events in their lives or reflecting on what they had been talking about, but actually with blank minds. Then Jim, remembering Andy's abortive Italian job, broke the reverie. Something had gone through his mind:

'Anyway, I'm only up for the Eurostar trips nowadays. Why go abroad, at least to the back of the beyond, Far East and whatnot? It's always misery. One of the great things about being old, in my view, old friend, is never having to see Heathrow again... Let's drink to that.' And they did. 'A few days in a civilised European city – in northern Europe, I mean – where you can get decent beer and food, and there're good art galleries and concert halls: that's enough for me. Why does anyone want to go to bleedin' Thailand, for God's sake? I don't get it.'

'I'm beginning to agree with you since...'

'If the prisons were half as awful as Heathrow, there'd be much less crime. If they were as bad as Luton, there'd soon be no crime at all.'

'You don't like Heathrow and Luton, then? I can hardly believe it.' Andy was used to humouring people, and banter came easily: though he had begun his working life in motor insurance, along with most of the others he was to meet that day, he did the "knowledge" when he was in his mid-twenties and had been a London taxi driver until he retired a year or two ago. The retirement was at least partly for health reasons; years of sitting in a taxi had taken a toll on his circulation and ticker. But it had given him a stock of jokes and skill in repartee. At the moment, however, he was not getting much opportunity.

'If prisons were as bad as Luton, there'd soon be no crime at all,' Jim repeated, lost in contemplation of his agenda for prison reform. The full horror of air travel, now he had started to think seriously about it again, had to be got off his chest, even though he was aware Andy was mocking him.

'You may laugh, but these airports, and the whole airport experience – parking, checking in, security, incarceration without crime for an indefinite time – why does anyone go through it who doesn't have to? It's not worth it, is it, just to see bloody Ayers Rock or Machu Picchu? Trouble is, Andy, though Maureen hasn't actually been everywhere, it's still on her list.'

'The others are late as well – as well as George, I mean,' Andy said.

'Yeah.'

'I take it then you're not going to Spain in December, as usual?'

'Oh – er – yes, we're off in the second week, I think; Madrid again,' Jim said, evidently embarrassed, fiddling with his spectacles and deciding his raincoat was in need of folding neatly.'

'But…'

'The wife, Maureen, wants to; it's a question of putting on a brave face and going along with it, or looking at Arkle for months.'

'Arkle?'

'The horse – long face. Geddit?'

'Oh, of course… It's a long way to go on a train though.'

'I should cocoa. Don't be daft. We're flying from Heathrow. Nothing to do with me.'

Jim drank deeply again. Andy looked at him incredulously, lost for words – unusual for a taxi driver. Jim saw the effect his hypocrisy had had, and playing the fool seemed the only way out:

'I vos only obeyink orders,' he said, putting on his pantomime blind-fanaticism face, the effect bolstered with a Nazi salute.

Jim was nearly through his first pint and was beginning to relax properly and, so far as he ever could nowadays, enjoy himself.

He was not fat enough to play Mr Pickwick – he merely had a modest beer belly – nor short enough; but when not morose – that meant, for example, when in a pub and things were nicely underway – there was often a facial resemblance to the jovial Pickwick. When Jim was happy, his cheeks and jowls, which were shaved to a marmoreal smoothness; his expression of warmth and tolerance (available to him only in pubs and after a couple had gone down); the almost bald head; and the rimless spectacles sitting so low on his nose that he had always to look over the top of them unless reading – all this combined to give him a jolly Pickwickian look. At least, from the neck up. First there was Jekyll and Hyde, here was Anderton and Pickwick.

Only recently his wife had arranged to collect Jim from a pub. She arrived and searched the bar with gimlet eyes and among its many patrons her attention was drawn particularly to a jovial, laughing, round-faced gentleman entertaining a group of half a dozen appreciative auditors in a dim corner. She strode past the happy, noisy scene twice before responding to a call: 'He's here, Mrs Anderton.' The entertainer was Jim, but not Jim as *she* knew him.

Winston and Ben, smartly dressed men for their age, entered the Slug and Lettuce together, just in time to catch sight of Jim finishing his mad Nazi routine.

'Jim's in form,' Ben said.

'Had a few already, I shouldn't wonder,' said Winston.

The pub was beginning to fill up and become noisy with law and bank workers, or whatever other jobs their nondescript suits might represent; all enjoying a brief respite from servitude.

'How wonderful not to be one of these poor buggers anymore,' Ben said, meaning that it was wonderful to be retired, secure, and beholden to none and responsible for no one – except the wife, of course.

Winston nodded. They knew they were lucky. Their pensions were not huge and their wealth not great, but retirement had come to them before the bottom fell out of the pensions market. They were happy in the knowledge that nothing short or Weimar Republic inflation could seriously impinge. Mortgages had been paid up long ago, investments were well spread, their pensions inflation-proofed, and sufficient wealth had been passed on to kick start the children's independent lives without demeaning the mother lode. Nonetheless, Winston felt constrained to spoil the mood – a contrarian thought had occurred to him:

'I dare say, Ben, if we were given the chance to be twenty again we'd grab it with both hands, but you could ask any twenty-year-old, and it wouldn't matter how much university and other debt he had hanging over him, he'd never swap places with an old geezer. What the twenty-year-old will never trade, I suspect, is hope and the decades of life experience before him, or her, of course, which we don't have any more.'

'I suppose you're right,' Ben said, 'in a choice between money or life, life always wins. Has to.'

When Ben and Winston got to the alcove table, it was guarded by Jim alone against many envious eyes. Andy, seeing Ben and Winston arrive, had gone to get a couple more pints while the latecomers fought their way through the crowd. The meeting between Ben and Winston and Jim, when it came, was low key. It had less in common with tunnellers connecting underground after years toiling from opposite sides of a massif than a meeting between householder and gas meter reader. Nods of bare recognition and nothing else. But it didn't imply indifference, not to them anyway.

'How's the prostate, Ben, old friend?' Jim asked cheerily, after preliminaries – only for conversation essentially; the last thing he wanted was chapter and verse. 'You'd better sit this side. Andy almost crippled himself getting out to go for your drinks,' and Jim moved as if to pull the table out for Winston before remembering it was a pointless action.

'Regular as clockwork – I can tell the time by it,' Ben said. 'I'm beginning to consider radical options: moving the bed into the bathroom, a holiday at Dignitas.'

Ben's prostate problem raised a smile and broke the ice of reunion, but Andy's return from the bar was uppermost in the minds of Winston and Ben. They had caught sight of Andy when they were at the door but couldn't now spot his fleshy, pasty, chicken-pox ravaged face among the throng of young people occupying the space between their alcove and the bar counter. Andy was a little less than medium height, so he might not be seen again until he emerged alcove-side. Winston and Ben each thought, though neither said anything, that he would be carrying only two pints, and therefore, unless he took a direct hit from a twit who was already far gone, he should get their pints through without spillage: most important.

The pub was now full, as always by this time on a weekday, and most drinkers had to stand. There were a few tables in the open space between the three walls of open alcoves and the bar, and there was chest-high shelving around the pillars in the open area. The bar itself stretched almost the whole length of the fourth wall. The alcove selected by Andy directly faced the bar, though when you were sitting down in it and the pub was full, you could not see the bar, only the top shelf behind it on which all the liquors the public never asked for were lined up. Three bar staff were constantly pouring drinks and settling up. All conversation among those standing in the open area had to be shouted to be heard; the alcoves had it a bit better in this respect. A drawback of the pub was the cellar lavatories, access to which was down a dangerously steep and narrow staircase: for the fat or infirm it was a daunting, Duke of Edinburgh award type of challenge.

Andy came through with the drinks unspilled but wincing from pain in his bunions, which was always worse in cold weather.

'Right, there we are guys – two pints,' Andy said, handing them over with great care, sweating at the exertion. 'I suppose George'll arrive as soon as I sit down, and I'll have to fight to the counter again for his pint. Why can't he ever get here on time? It's not that hard, is it?'

For some reason George was often late for these get-togethers, or any appointment – in fact, it would be more accurate to say he was usually late; it could be anything between fifteen minutes and three quarters of an hour in the case of these lunchtime booze-ups. Today, he was twenty minutes late so far, and still fifteen minutes away, at the very least; that is, from the moment he discovered his mistake and set off for the right pub.

George was late today because he was in the Nell Gwynne, in Bull Inn Court off the Strand, a drinking hole always used by him and his friends to round off after their monthly Oldie Magazine literary lunches at Simpson's in the Strand (so-called "literary", but more likely to feature a celebrity chef than a Booker Prize winner). He had gone there today on autopilot and for ten minutes had been wondering why no one else had turned up. Then it flashed upon him that he was in the wrong place and had better get a taxi to the Slug and Lettuce, and quickly. Walking was not an option: too much drinking time would be lost doing the Strand and Fleet Street on foot, and, more important, the later his appearance at the S and L the greater the abuse to be faced when he got there.

Leaving the Nell Gwynne and his half-quaffed pint, he turned right and walked the few yards under an arch which brought him to the Strand. Emerging from the narrow and reeking alleyway in which this treasure of a bygone age is hidden, he just had time, while hailing a taxi, to read and chuckle at the small blackboard the pub had placed against the wall at the junction of alleyway and Strand. The board constituted the pub's sole and unique way of advertising its obscure existence to the larger world in which the Strand participated. Its chalked legend, changed daily, today read: 'Have you been injured in a workplace accident? No? Well, you're not drinking enough at lunchtime. Let us help you win compensation.' Just our kind of pub, George thought: *Why do we ever go anywhere else?*

George was tall and thin, with a shock of wavy white hair which was frizzled around the ears and neck. On his long narrow head and face the skin hung loosely, as if the skull had shrunk with age, or he had some bloodhound in his ancestry; but his eyes were always sharp and intelligent, despite his memory lapses and increasing absentmindedness of late. He attributed this woolly-headedness, which was how he thought of it, to his declining interest in what was going on in the world, both the world at large and his particular social whirl – present company he was about to meet excepted. The declining interest itself he assumed to be an inevitable feature of old age.

Unusually, the Strand and Fleet Street were reasonably clear of traffic and George got to the Slug and Lettuce in another ten minutes. His arrival was met with a barrage of abuse from his friends for his lateness, and then some open ridicule when he was unwise enough to explain the true reason for his delay. The earlier message to Andy about the Central Line being up the creek had been just a tactic when it looked to George as though he would be late for the Nell Gwynne.

Chapter 2

It was not too long before they were all seated with pints in front of them, and now needing only to think of something to say to each another. Andy and Winston were jammed behind the table, and the other three had relative comfort and freedom in the easy chairs that Jim had called "Queen Anne things".

When the cursory greetings, abuse and ridicule were done with, it was Andy who started the ball rolling:

'I had my six-month check-up recently and they told me I could still drink in moderation – whatever that means – but I should avoid excitement. So I reckon you lot are still the ideal company: I don't think any of us has excited anyone in the last half a century.'

'You're flattering us,' Winston said, laughing, straightening his trousers' creases as he did so and adjusting the knot of his tie, 'you could go back a lot further than fifty years.'

Winston Cryer – well into his seventies of course – was on the albino side of blond, with about half the wavy hair now that he had had in his twenties; his cerulean blue eyes and nearly white eyelashes and eyebrows gave him a Bond villain look, which was enhanced by his slightly aloof manor. He was of medium height, slim still, possibly because he "worked out", and went on ski holidays rather than cruises; and he dressed sharply for his age, as if still operating as a marine insurance broker and needing to impress clients that he was good enough at his job to have made a pile for himself. He retained a habit acquired when working and regularly wearing expensive suits, of always straightening his trousers' creases when sitting down, and he had an OCD frequency of checking his tie knot. Years of alcohol-based lunches when working in the Lloyd's Insurance Market had left him with a lot of pinkish red blotches on his face; so many blotches that his face resembled, in colour predominance, the world map before the British Empire dissolved: a dissolution that would have been more or less complete only a few years after Winston was born.

'George turning up late after being at the wrong pub reminds me of when Les was at the Coach and Horses in Soho and we were all at the Chandos,' Winston said. 'You and Ben were there that night,' he said, looking unintentionally villain-like, first at George and Ben across the table and then at Andy beside him, for confirmation of his story.

They nodded and Ben said:

'It was a typical Les cockup. We all had a couple at the Chandos, waiting for him, and someone then had the idea – God knows why – that Les must've made a mistake and gone to the Coach and Horses. No mobiles then, so we decided to traipse up there, stopping for one at the Salisbury on the way. You don't know this, I suppose, Jim, because you weren't with us that night...'

'No, I wasn't,' Jim put in, 'but I've heard the story a dozen times over the past forty years...while you were all on the way to the Coach and Horses, Les was on his way to the Chandos. Am I right?'

Jim adjusted his specs: moved them up a bit and back to where they were; and then he patted his scanty hair in a surprisingly dandyish way for an old codger, as if reassuring himself it was still there and tidy.

'Yes, but...' Ben began, stroking his shaved bald pate; this movement with both hands, from front to back, was a reflex when his temper was aroused, which happened easily and this time was triggered by Jim's put down.

'Is he still alive, do you think?' George interrupted.

'Must be dead.'

'Must be.'

'Couldn't still be alive.'

Jim shed some light: 'I think we were the last to see him – Tony and me, that is – and that would be well over thirty, or thirty-five years ago. We went down to Hernia Bay for a day. There was no way you'd get him up to London by then, even though he was only in his thirties. Christ, what a dump Herne Bay is – was even then...'

'What was he doing there – I mean, for a living?' Andy asked.

They were all listening, not with rapt intent, but their faces did have a special look: something of the look, say, of credulous film buffs imbibing the reminiscences of the last intimates of James Dean.

'That's where he came from, old friend,' Jim answered. 'His parents lived there, though I'm not sure whether they were still alive when Tony and I went to see him – either of them.'

'Didn't you ask where he was living or anything?' Ben questioned.

'No, I don't think we did. I don't remember. That's one of the ways we change, I suppose.

'Nowadays, the first thing we so-called property owners want to know is always "where do you live?" –isn't it? Either he was still with his parents or he'd inherited the house, I suppose – bungalow actually.'

'What did you do in Herne Bay – for a whole day?' Ben asked. The others were still listening, leaning forwards to catch everything, because of the pub noise.

'Just walked about the place, saw all the EU funding signs – or perhaps that's false memory – had a few beers in places Les must've thought were the best Herne Bay had to offer – a sandwich lunch in one of them. One or two people nodded to him as we strolled around. He took us to an amusement arcade – yes, it's coming back to me now; he'd been working for a time in the arcade, collecting the money, whatever, supervising. He'd even asked the local council, so he told us, and he did this without any embarrassment mind, whether they'd pay him to clean up the litter on the promenade. Which they wouldn't. So there was no real work around. Why would there be in a place like that?'

'And that was it?'

'Doesn't sound like a whole day.'

'Did you get drunk?'

'We didn't get drunk, old friend. For some reason we were only drinking halves. It seems odd looking back on it. Les was pleased to see us but we both felt, Tony and me, he'd be glad when it was over; we were part of the life he was done with. It wouldn't happen again. He still went along with all our old jokes – did the tense, juddering British Army salute, for instance, when we left at the railway station. That's the last I remember of the day: us looking out of the carriage window, him exaggeratedly standing at attention on the platform with his saluting hand vibrating at his forehead, a hugely fat figure, his blazer ready to burst its buttons, and an inane grin on his face. God moves in mysterious ways, hey?'

They all pictured the scene for a few moments.

'Sounds like a gay version of *Brief Encounter*,' Andy suggested.

That earned a laugh, and Jim took the punchline break as cue to get another round in. But before going to the bar he wanted to be the one to finish the story, his story, so he added his own conclusion:

'We've all written him off because we don't like the idea of him living the rest of his life independently of us. For all we know, he might be alive, or could be anyway, and the rich owner of Herne Bay's first vape shop. God moves in mysterious ways, as I say too often, especially for an atheist.'

'Might be running a Christian mission in wherever,' Ben laughed.

'Or be Giorgio Armani's chief designer,' one of the others added.

Winston said: 'It's funny that we'd always be going to the pub that Les liked, or leaving one he decided he didn't like. But he wasn't what you'd call an Alpha male, was he, or even intelligent above the average? Outside the pub environment – a word we'd never have used in Les' day, *environment*, not in that context – he was passive, happy-go-lucky, as I remember him: mad on cricket, Kent cricket especially.'

'That's true,' Andy said, 'most nights we'd end up drinking in Villiers Street or in the bar at Charing Cross, only because that was Les' station. Bugger that the rest of us were going home from Paddington or Liverpool Street, or wherever. It's Les' fault that my feet are in such a state, all those nights in the winter walking back from Charing Cross to Liverpool Street in leaky winkle pickers.'

Andy took the moment to loosen the Velcro on his ancient trainers, footwear grossly incongruent with his habitual blazer and grey flannels but all that he could bear on his feet nowadays.

George laughed – particularly George but the others also – as he had still lived in Clapton at the time with his parents, the time being the early swinging sixties, of course. (Except that for most working-class boys who started work at sixteen as insurance clerks all the swinging passed them by – happened elsewhere rather). When Les was taking his leave from Charing Cross to get the last or a late train to Herne Bay, as George fondly remembered it, he himself still had to get to a 22 bus and endure a tortuous journey through east London, a bus loaded with drunks – fellow drunks. Les would get to Herne Bay before he got to Clapton.

George smiled at the recollection of the days of youthful vitality; often when the 22 bus got to its terminus at the top of Chatsworth Road, he would buy a bag of chips and, after first saturating them in malt vinegar and snowfalling them with salt, eat them whilst walking down Chats to where he lived at the bottom end of Powerscroft Road. If he had been drinking with the lads straight from work, from five o'clock onwards and probably at the Bell off Cannon Street, he might be strolling down Chats as early as nine or ten o'clock in the evening. In which case, as he now recalled, there was always the risk that Uncle Bill and Aunt Gladys had called at 159 Powerscroft Road, his parents' house, bringing with them his Grandmother for a dreaded unannounced visit.

Ancient Nanna lived in Liverpool but from time to time came to stay with her daughter Gladys and son-in-law Bill, who lived in Finchley. In those days, when coming home early, before entering the ancestral pile young George would check the cars parked in the road nearby – never many of them in those days – looking for the huge Vauxhall that Uncle Bill drove. If he saw it, it confirmed a visit by the family with Nanna.

George would then keep walking in a circling pattern, taking in Millfields Road, Saratoga Road and Mayola Road, like an aircraft waiting for a landing slot, until the disappearance of the Vauxhall signalled the end of the visit. Young George, old George remembered, just did not want to deal with all the how-are-you-getting-on, any-girlfriends-yet, that's-a-nice-haircut, tell-'em-about-your-salary-increase, give Nanna-a-kiss-George, stuff. The small front room would be charged with love and admiration and expectation, all directed at him – the next generation, the torch bearer – and he had no way of dealing with it, and no desire to find one.

George smiled broadly at the memory of this youngster, for whom, naturally enough, he felt a strong attachment, and when he smiled the vertical lines of the folds of excess flesh on his intelligent, usually serious long face, were pulled aside in the middle; it was like heavy velvet curtains being tied back; the effect was transformational – from Bertrand Russell to Harpo Marx. It was the shock of white hair that made the comparison compelling, though when these guys referred to it, as they still did sometimes, one of them was sure to point out that hardly anyone else in the pub would know what either Russell or Marx – still talking about Harpo – looked like.

'Good days, though,' George said, 'our best days in many ways.' He was referring to the recollections of Les, of course, but also to his old life in Powerscroft Road with his parents and elder brother, and the graceless youth who could not cope with aunts, uncles and grandparent.

Jim was now in sight, holding a tray of five pints with great care, and the crowd warily giving him way, fearful that the limping old codger might tip the lot given the least excuse.

Jim had been mouthing something repeatedly from the moment he could see that the others saw him coming. What it was he was mouthing none could make out, but all wondered what was so important it couldn't wait until he was back on a Queen Anne chair.

Still making the exaggerated Orangutan mouth movements as he put the tray down, Jim then switched from silent movie to talkie: 'Near twenty-five pounds for five pints. Five pounds each!'

'We can work the maths, Jim,' Winston said, doing his best to make it light-hearted, not sinister. He tried not to blink as he spoke, knowing from experience that his white eyelashes on the blink were always disconcerting. But he could not resist fiddling unnecessarily with his tie knot, and anyway his blue stare was as disconcerting as his blinking. He was slightly nervous that his quip would be taken as an insult rather than a joke.

'Time to visit aunty's,' Ben announced, 'bloody prostate.'

The others said nothing, and they all avoided eye contact with each other for a minute. It was a bit like that moment, scaled down of course, when Oates announced to Captain Scott and the others that he was going outside and might be a while. Ben got up and moved off to the lavatory, "aunty's" being the group's euphemism for same; it was a usage imported into the company which they all worked for by another of their number who joined the insurer in the sixties, Rob Davies, and it stuck. It fitted the propensity of the young men to play language games – anybody who was anybody in the company was given a nickname. Rob Davies himself soon after joining was known as "The President" because of his facial resemblance to Jack Kennedy. Only after their retirement did the nicknames gradually fade from use between them.

Ben made a joke of his dodgy prostate – what else could he do? If you are in a pub with friends and you get up to go to the loo with absurd frequency, you have to take a public position on it – they, the friends, will not ignore your semi incontinence.

In Ben's case, he had been coping with his prostate condition for a few years now, during which the gamut of treatment options had been tried on him – chemotherapy, radiotherapy and a couple of operations to remove chunks of the offending gland.

His life had changed since the diagnosis. It proved to be his climacteric. Old age had come to him in such a way that he could not deny it to himself or, worse in some ways, to others about him. His prostate made him retire from Lloyd's earlier than he would have chosen; his appetite for gym workouts dried up; he was now undeniably fat; his social life, much of which had always revolved around sports, either as participant or spectator, was circumscribed for the future by the demands of a bladder constantly under pressure from the prostate's insatiable territorial demands. He had become short tempered. At his home in Shenfield in Essex, his French wife, Brigitte, came in for the brunt of his irritability, and the irritability was extended to his three girls whenever he saw them. Ben could not help reflecting on the irreversible decline since his glory days as winner of amateur boxing trophies. Those were the days, he would often say to himself nowadays when on the way to the nearest urinal, where he would spend quite a while looking down and concentrating on not splashing his trousers.

Nothing had turned out as he had hoped. He had failed in his career. Starting out from humble beginnings, there was never any expectation of great success, but there came a time when it looked as though he might become the underwriter of a decent Lloyd's motor insurance syndicate. His expectations grew; he and his wife made plans; in the event, it came to no more than deputy underwriter of a so-so syndicate. Now he was comfortably well-off but fat, old, bald, broken-nosed, a near alcoholic and permanently in hock to the lavatory. 'Otherwise life's just grand,' he laughed to himself while standing at a Slug and Lettuce urinal enjoying one of the last true bodily pleasures left him – urinating. It took a hell of a time, of course, but the end result left him more satisfied and relaxed than almost anything else could these days. But not for long.

I can't have any more beer he decided, climbing back up to the bar; I don't want to be doing this too often today. I've been up ladders less steep. I'll switch to G and T's.

When Ben was safely out of earshot on the way to the loo, Winston had said, 'There but for the grace of God and all that.'

'We haven't necessarily escaped, old friend,' Jim said, 'maybe it's just not our time – yet.' He drank deeply of his next pint.

'Looks like we're all going out with a whimper not a bang,' George said. 'We're all running down like old mechanical clocks.'

'For sure, at the end there'll be no bang,' Andy smirked. 'Certainly no bang,' he reiterated, making sure the double entendre hadn't been missed. 'More's the pity.

'Much more likely I'll be whimpering over my feet when my turn comes.'

Andy then stretched lethargically before again loosening the Velcro on his trainers. He broke out into a sweat, breathed heavily and scrabbled for a tissue to dab the porridge-like skin of his face.

'Sometime lads…sometime, we should arrange to meet and all go out with a bang,' Winston said. 'All jump off the Shard, or some such.'

He blinked. But they were used to it.

'Jesus,' Ben said, collapsing gratefully into his seat again: 'What's all this about jumping off the Shard? How could you? Wouldn't you just slide – fast?'

Jim explained: 'We're discussing whether we should go quietly or kick over the traces before we snuff it... You know – rage against the dying of the light, and all that stuff. Though in Dylan Thomas's case the rage, his rage, was nothing more than drinking himself to death, wasn't it?'

'We're on the right lines then,' Andy said, demonstrating by taking a large swig.

'There's a difference of degree that's significant, Andy, as Jim knows,' Winston explained, hand on tie knot. 'Dylan Thomas's binges were on a scale that dwarfs our polite gatherings. We get a bit merry and have a mild hangover in the morning; he drank insanely. He insulted, picked fights, vomited, collapsed, urinated on carpets; was thrown out of pubs, homes, hotels or got carried out unconscious...'

'Sounds like the sort of life you led Winston, when you were twenty,' Andy said.

The others laughed, pleased to be reminded that they had their good times once. Heard the chimes at midnight, as it were.

'Going out with a bang, old friend,' Jim said, 'in my books at any rate, means having a swipe at all the things you've hated but been unable to do anything about. Doing it just before you intend to top yourself. And by swipe, mind, I mean something serious: murder most foul, as they say.'

'Who though?'

'The candidates present themselves only too obviously,' Jim said with relish, '– present company excepted, of course. For instance, there they are lined up from the worlds of politics, television, fashion, film, business. Celebs. An embarrassment of choice.'

'It's a nice idea, Jim,' George said, 'but difficult in the execution: getting at a prime minister, say, if that's your choice, is nigh impossible nowadays...'

'Too many people want to do it,' Andy quipped.

George gave his Harpo Marx grin. 'My own preference would be for something like the five of us skydiving together from thirty thousand feet wearing faulty parachutes.'

'Yes, and shouting, "Goodbye cruel world,"' Andy suggested.

'That's going out with a cliché, not a bang,' said George.

Chapter 3

Within the space of a few years, starting in 1958, all five men attending this fateful get-together began their careers with the Minster Insurance Company. Winston and Andy joined straight from school at age sixteen in 1959; Jim had joined in 1958 from school when Tony, Les, Bob and Terry began – the four mates now dead who made up the larger group of earlier times; three certainly dead, Les, as mentioned, missing in action and presumed dead. Tony, Bob and Terry would have been at the Slug and Lettuce if alive.

The other two among the still living, Ben and George, briefly had employment elsewhere before joining Minster, where the lure for young men without impressive academic qualifications, a lure hard to resist in those days, was the promise of a salary scale that took you to a thousand pounds a year at the tender age of thirty. And it *was* tender in those days, though today a thirty-year old might well be running a hedge fund or an airline. George's first job was in local government at Hackney Town Hall, where there seemed no likelihood of earning a thousand a year at any age. Ben got his first employment from the London Electricity Board – clerical, stunningly dull even by the standards of clerking, and badly paid.

Minster Insurance Company, where all these youngsters came to know one another, was a respected and soundly managed company, formed in the early nineteen fifties. It specialised in motor insurance and operated from a detached post-war office block in Arthur Street, by London Bridge – an undistinguished building, but it had the saving grace of being next door to the renowned and still surviving El Vino wine bar in Martin Lane, the interior of which in the fifties needed no adjustment to satisfy anyone wishing to film Dickens in an authentic setting.

It is worth mentioning that Minster was soundly run because some of its competitors were not: Vehicle and General, and Fire, Auto and Marine were two insurance companies whose mushroom speed of growth ended in the mid nineteen sixties in spectacular financial crashes – financial disasters that became front page national newspaper stories. In the case of the ill-starred Fire, Auto and Marine, its swindler and fraudster boss, Emil Savundra, made a famous appearance on television's The Frost Programme. The Frost versus Savundra interview came to be described as a trial by television, an expression that remains current in the language. Savundra was arrested in 1967, found guilty in 1968, and sentenced to eight years' imprisonment.

The financial world was no less corrupt then than now, despite the ubiquity in the fifties, and still in the early sixties, of that symbol of City respectability – the bowler hat. When Winston, Jim, Andy, George and Ben started working in the City, arriving at Liverpool Street, or London Bridge, or Fenchurch Street, or wherever, their first and unexpected sight of an army of dark suits topped with bowlers had been intimidating. It spoke to them – dimly of course because of their inexperience and unworldliness – of continuity, responsibility, probity, self-confident ancient institutions, treasured values held in trust across the generations, a man's word being his bond – all baloney of course, as it turned out.

All our young men, except for Ben and George, got their jobs at Minster, as mentioned, straight from school after O levels, by responding to Evening Standard advertisements which sought bright school leavers wanting a secure career in insurance – luncheon vouchers worth three shillings a day, one Saturday morning work per month, two weeks holiday a year, excellent prospects and attractive salary scale.

In those days, a young man, working-class, with meagre academic qualifications, need not mull over a prospect like that. Excepting George, perhaps, whose mother nevertheless somehow intuited that he had not found his metier in Hackney Town Hall's post department. She understood that he needed fresh woods and pastures new. George was not doing anything about it, so his mother saw that it was down to her. She discovered the Minster advertisement, which frequently appeared in London's evening newspapers, and drew it to the attention of the languishing George. He managed to write a basic application letter, after much cajoling, conveying that he was indeed a bright school leaver who wanted a secure career in insurance. The rest is history.

Ben also was drawn to the City, after his false start of half a year at the London Electricity Board, by the lure of more pound notes; though in those days the Minster lads often converted their monthly salary cheque at the counter of Williams Deacons Bank, off King William Street, into ten-shilling notes – because the wad you came away with would be twice as thick.

Apropos cashing cheques, the story is kept alive by re-telling from time to time at the old geezers' lunch meetings, of how Les, handing his first pay cheque over the bank counter for conversion, was asked by a dignified Chamberlain-collared cashier (these types could still be found in the sixties) how he wanted to receive his money.

'In cash, please,' was Les' answer.

Each of our unfamous five would have recognised his earlier self – no doubt, but not without embarrassment at the gauche and boorish behaviour of his youthful persona, or anxiety over the unlikely prospect he presented of making any kind of headway in the world; certainly, if it depended on nothing but the power of his own hands pulling on his own bootstraps.

Teenage Jim, who has been described when in his Pickwickian seventies as tall, pot-bellied, scant of hair, lame in the left leg, bespectacled, round-faced, and usually morose when not in a pub, joined Minster as a lean and lanky, athletic, happy youth with dense unkempt brown hair and an enthusiasm for new experience, new friendships.

He was an only child, brought up in Muswell Hill, who had played cricket for his school and enjoyed being a scout; in later life he had become a scout leader, for which he was frequently ribbed by his friends; it was as if he had admitted to a love of crocheting or singing madrigals. He had never ordered a drink in a pub until he started work, but once he broke his duck – in his first week – he was never called on to prove he had reached the legal age despite looking younger than he was. He had been to a boys' secondary school, so his experience of girls when he joined Minster was nil. But girls in those days were employed by the bushel in insurance companies as shorthand typists and secretaries. The vision of ten or twenty girls aged between sixteen and twenty-five corralled in a typing pool, their manual typewriters rarely silent and very noisy when in use, was something he woke up thinking about every morning. He walked past the pool as often as he could find reason to, every working day.

'You again, Anderton?' the deputy managing director of Minster would say to Jim when they sometimes met in passing the typing pool. His question would be accompanied by an understanding though admonishing twinkle in his eye. It was headmasterly, and indeed the atmosphere at Minster was not much different from school; most of the trainee underwriters were under twenty-five, and the majority of these were under twenty; they would routinely and quite naturally – that is to say, without condescension – be called "lad" by the management; that or "boy": the "management" being men in their forties or fifties who had, most of them, done their bit on the Normandy beaches, or in Italy or North Africa or elsewhere.

"Old" Jim was aware of how different it was now and felt a tinge of pity for today's youngsters. As far as he could see, they were expected to be adult from the day they switched from school, or university, to work. Tough.

Jim's aforementioned deputy managing director, Stanley Rogers, a huge man both in height and bulk, and a chain-smoking eczema sufferer, would catch Jim on an unnecessary stroll whilst on one of his own rarer peregrinations. These walks of Mr Rogers were carried out, as all the young trainee underwriters knew, partly for work reasons but, undoubtedly, also for supervisory purposes – a policeman's beat, as it were; the policeman's beat being a custom the purpose and regularity of which Jim's generation could still remember. Young men who were still schoolboys in spirit bore no strong grudge against schoolmasters for "policing" them.

On one summer day, early afternoon, when they must both have been in their late teens, perhaps even twenty by then, Jim and Tony Turner had been improvising a two-man cricket match in one of the long open spaces between the tall filing cabinets which occupied the basement of Minster House. Just high spirits: no more requiring explanation than the play of kittens. As Tony was bowling a screwed-up ball of paper at Jim, just as fast as he could from a short run-up, and Jim was swiping and missing with a wooden hand brush that served as a bat, who should turn up but Mr Rogers. He was looking for a lost file and checking that it had not been miss-filed by the filing girls (of course they *were* all girls for such a menial task) – the usual checks would be whether a file had been misplaced by ten, or a hundred, or a thousand places.

'Nothing better to do, lads? No work?' Mr Rogers said, rummaging through various slender cardboard files, cigarette ash tumbling here, there and everywhere from the fag in the corner of his mouth.

It was all he needed to say. The boys – very much boys now – scuttled off to their desks upstairs and kept their heads down, and their tails between their legs.

They had been unlucky. Most afternoons the management – comprising the peripatetic Mr Rogers, the managing director himself Jimmy Wilson, and one or two lesser figures – would down pens at around twelve thirty, light a new cigarette for the journey, and stroll the fifty yards to El Vino for their lunch.

No one knew what they had for lunch – though pubs and wine bars were not big on food in those days: for the most part they set out to do what it said on the tin – so it is reasonable to believe it was mainly alcohol. No one knew, however, since no one else at Minster had the courage to venture into El Vino when the management were there.

Wilson and Rogers, and whoever might be with them, Mr Cullen perhaps, known to the lads as Snaggers for his frequent use of the expression "the snag is" – the El Vino lunch group often did not return until three o'clock, or thereabouts, and always they would file back like Dunkirk evacuees disembarking back in Blighty: unsteady on the feet, vague faces, dishevelled, and fags hanging on the lip; more Bogart-style now than Ronald Coleman.

Tony and Jim were right to feel unlucky that day they were caught in the basement playing cricket.

Jim often thought about that incident – down the years it kept coming back to mind unbidden, fresh and vivid, and always causing him to smile. But so much else had happened over the decades that had not really registered with him. Or perhaps the memories had been miss-filed, ten or a hundred, or a thousand places, never to be found again.

There were many other memories of his early life at Minster that Jim could summon up, though it irritated him that none of them seemed to possess any particular significance. It rankled with Jim whenever he heard people on radio or television going on about never being able to forget where they were at the height of the Cuban Missile Crisis – people of his own age. It rankled because no matter how hard he tried he could never recall anything about his own doings at the time. He had been dimly aware that Cuba was in the news, and America and Russia were rowing about it. But that was all; the Crisis had not made enough impression on him for it to become permanently fixed in his mind and inseparably associated, as a memory, with whatever else then had been happening to him.

But who knows whether our memories really have any other significance than to remind us who we are; or knows what items, after all, from the baggage train of memories that drags behind us, actually matter – could not, that is, be shed without damage? All thoughts, these, that Jim often pondered when alone walking, or just alone. Once, in a pub, he got talking to George about it and all George said was, 'I hope they don't matter too much – your memories – because mine seem to be on the wane: names, appointments, whatever – I forget everything these days… So long as I still know who I am, hey.'

The heart has its reasons, of which reason knows nothing, Jim remembered from somewhere. It made him think that perhaps memories have their purposes, which neither reason nor the heart can hope to understand.

My memories, Jim reflected as he grew older, – those events, incidents, people that my mind chooses to keep on record, without asking permission, and which it then interrupts me with at the oddest of times – they're what have made me what I am, I suppose. In a sense they *are* me – without them I cease to exist. No memories, no person. Alzheimer's. But why these memories and not others? Other things did happen to me – more important things, I'm sure. To what purpose the accumulation of all that trivia, and little whose particular significance, for me at any rate, is obvious? Just to create this miserable clapped out old sod that stands before you? I wonder. I should cocoa.

That is how it would go. "I should cocoa" being a favourite although now hopelessly dated expression of Jim's, like his "old friend". "God moves in mysterious ways" would be Jim's usual way of winding up when he had gone as far as he could with his speculations, always intending with it contempt for the Supreme Being's planning and execution. An "Ah, well..." and a sigh would sum it up, often enough, finally.

On one occasion when he was running through these thoughts about memory, he found himself lip-speaking, without realising it, his train of thought having caused him to remember a couple of lines of T S Eliot that seemed relevant: *But to what purpose, disturbing the dust on a bowl of rose-leaves, I do not know.* To what purpose indeed, mate; I should cocoa.

English poetry was a love of Jim's, a pleasure that had grown steadily over the years, so that he would now rather take a selection of Browning on holiday than a novel. Not something he would ever talk about with his friends.

Jim often remembered a Christmas Eve after-work festive drink with the lads – and some girls from the office too, thanks be. Feeling he had had enough to drink by about seven o'clock; however, he decided to make his way home. Walking along Cannon Street with this objective in his hazy mind he felt an arm slip under his own arm and, as it were, hang on pleasantly. It was Patricia, the girl who had been allocated to be his shorthand typist: the girl to whom for the past few weeks he had been dictating badly composed letters; letters to insurance brokers in the main – dull stuff, but the core of the work.

Jim was flattered by Pat's friendly act – it was the first time any girl had taken an initiative of that kind with him, and he certainly liked it. She had also had a drink or two, no doubt.

'Are you off home, then, Jim?' she smiled at him as she asked.

'Yes, I live in Muswell Hill – not very exciting,' Jim replied, happy feeling her arm under his and through it all her youthful lightness, buoyancy. 'And you?'

'I live in Southend now, but we're moving to Walthamstow in London soon – my dad's changing jobs.'

'I like Southend. I've been there a few times. Are you going home there now?'

'Yes.'

'I'll come too, shall I? – there's time for me to get back,' Jim said recklessly.

Pat laughed but raised no objections.

They got a train from Fenchurch Street – so far as Jim could remember it *was* Fenchurch Street, but it could just as easily have been Liverpool Street; false memory and all that. Whatever station it was, he forgot to get a ticket, but on Christmas Eve, the barrier checks were lax, and it was not noticed by the depleted contingent of railway staff at either end of the line.

How Jim and Patricia decided on the next step he had no recollection, but the two of them, he knew, were at some stage in the evening sitting next to each other watching *Spartacus* in a Southend cinema. Then he must have fallen asleep (again?) towards the end of this epic of Roman brutality and paean to Kirk Douglas's muscles. He remembered it was near the end because the last thing he was conscious of was that everybody was claiming to be Spartacus. He did not wake up until the very patient Pat decided it was time to bring the revels to an end, and roused him. Once the two of them were outside the cinema – getting there a somewhat disorienting experience for the drowsy Jim – and breathing the fresh and invigorating sea air, Pat wished Jim a merry Christmas and pointed him towards the railway station.

One of Jim's many stumbles on his journey home, a journey involving night buses and a last, or "milk" train, was the origin, so Jim ever after believed, of his dodgy knee. It had not felt too bad at the time but with the dawning of the next day came the first of many bouts of extreme pain: in my beginning is my end.

Whatever became of that slim girl, Jim often wondered. If, after the passing of decades, she saw me in the distance in a shopping mall, she'd probably avoid me – and I'd do the same, I suppose. And for some reason which I don't understand, I think we'd be right to do so.

Each of the other old geezers could have recalled similar tales from their youth and early employment, and they sometimes shared them in sympathetic company. They still used the word sympathy, though nowadays it has been replaced by empathy.

Though Andy – fleshy, pasty-faced, pockmarked, and snub-nosed in youth as in old age – had left Minster in his mid-twenties to become a London taxi driver, and had the usual fund of taxi driver stories always at hand, his most vivid memories were of his first job and the first friends made after leaving school. For Andy, as for many of his work friends, the office was where he met his first girlfriend; for some of the friends it was where they met their wives to be – for one, though, Winston as it happens, it was only his first wife to be.

In youth Winston's albino blondness, blue eyes and athletic figure – long before the facial blotchiness – was strikingly handsome. He was the first to marry, a Minster shorthand typist, but it did not last; after five mostly unhappy and also childless years he was divorced. He did not marry again until in his late thirties.

Ben could remember clearly the day he met his future wife in a lunchtime restaurant in Plantation house, near Fenchurch Street station. It was in the winter of 1965; she was a waitress – a French waitress. Her voice, accent, her whole manner of bearing herself – aside from her youthful prettiness – were more than enough to justify Ben's unvarying lunch routine for the coming weeks: same restaurant, same time, same table, or one that she served. At that time Ben had not sustained his broken nose – that was a boxing injury he took on a year or two later. So, though short in height, but with hair in those days, he was an eligible young man, especially in a smart suit: suits were the mandated office wear. Brigitte thought he was eligible, that was all that mattered.

George, when he thought about his early days at Minster, remembered most fondly his closest friend, Tony Turner, the aforementioned cricketing partner of Jim. The two always laughed when in one another's company, and, in especial, they both took delight in what was risible about British films of that era. In quest of satisfying their curious hobby, they would visit every week the Essoldo cinema in Mare Street, Hackney, situated near the junction with Wells Street – a cinema long gone now. This cinema was independent in so far as it did not replicate the programming schedules of any other cinema known to man.

It would show Hammer Horror films, of course, and these would be backed by appallingly badly made and woodenly acted crime films, usually those introduced by the sinister and lugubrious Edgar Lustgarten, criminologist. If it were not showing a Hammer film, but there was something else available starring the wonderfully over the top camp Vincent Price – who went almost as far as to wink at the audience when embarking on the dastardly – then the Essoldo would get hold of it.

Any film with monsters in it would likely get a showing, no matter how inferior; crude sci-fi movies were regulars – and if there was a sci-fi film with monsters in it *and* Vincent Price starring, the Essoldo management's cup would be running all over the place. Just occasionally, the Essoldo would feature a torrid sex film – "torrid" being the adjective always used in those days to sell a film in which there was deemed to be a degree of sexual explicitness; albeit nowadays the film would get a PG rating without demur.

George could still laugh out aloud when he remembered one particular night at the Essoldo. The main film was Blood of the Vampire, starring Sir Donald Wolfit. While the boys were watching and enjoying this gory absurdity – and enjoying it precisely because of its gory absurdity – the cinema manager, a familiar of theirs after so many visits by them, walked up the aisle, surveying his domain; as he passed by George and Tony in their gangway seats, and recognised them in the semi dark, he smiled and asked whether they were enjoying themselves. They were, they said. 'Good,' the manager said. 'What we try to offer every week is good wholesome family entertainment. I'm glad it seems to be working.' George and Tony laughed for most of the rest of the evening, much of which they spent speculating on what other films might be categorised as "family entertainment" if Blood of the Vampire, and an insanely bloodthirsty Wolfit, qualified as a film for the family.

Chapter 4

George fought his way to the bar and got another round of pints to keep the ball rolling. By the time he arrived at the counter he had forgotten that Ben actually wanted a gin and tonic. It had been a struggle pushing his way through the packed crowd; the pub was as full as it could be, though soon the call of the office would begin the thinning out. George assumed that the effort to get to the bar and his anxiety over how to get the drinks back to their table without too much spillage was why he had cocked it up. That was what he would tell them anyway, having remembered Ben's changed order only half way through his return journey. And for sure he would offer, as sincerely as he could fake, to go back and get Ben's G and T. It would be taking a bit of a risk but he was confident that none of his friends was bastard enough to take up such an offer, in such circumstances.

When the offer *was* made, Winston intervened; he had always been fond of George and something was now troubling him about his friend. *Probably the poor old bugger's just getting drunk faster, as you do in old age,* he thought. In any event, Winston jumped up and suggested he get the G and T now, with the next round, which he would get on his way back from aunty's – or rather two G and T's to keep things straight. The offer was decently quashed by Ben who was glad to fall behind on the drinks tally without having to go through the humiliation of openly declining a drink.

George had helped Winston at a critical point in his career; they had been friends before that, but at this critical stage in Winston's career George had shown that he was prepared to go beyond the call of routine friendship to help Winston get a job he particularly wanted. George himself had left motor insurance when in his thirties and in partnership with an insurance broker friend started an employment agency specialising in insurance.

When Winston decided that he must do something other than motor insurance or go mad, it was George's employment agency that steered him towards marine insurance and made sure that all the competitors for the particular job Winston wanted (a low rung on the ladder merely, it has to be said) were worse prospects than him.

There was a lull and pause in the conversation, all of the old men filled it by looking vaguely around at the different groups in the pub. It was very different nowadays: nobody smoking, groups of women on their own and glad to be, a clientele less representative of society than it would have been in the old days. Years ago, Jim remembered, there were always old guys and men in workmen's clothing drinking pints of mild and coughing raucously between fags; everyone now, however, was, or looked, between twenty-five and sixty (present company excepted), and they all looked as if when they left the pub they might be returning to the same office and the same desktop arrangement of computers. Jim remembered pubs in the Monument area where at lunchtime there would be office staff, Billingsgate workers, scaffolders who were working on the rebuilding of Cannon Street station, street corner newspaper vendors – *not quite a microcosm of olde England,* Jim thought, *but a damn site closer than anything ever found now.*

'Have you noticed how everyone looks at us nowadays as if we shouldn't really be here because we're too old,' Andy said. He had noticed, as had the others, that, as usual, at least half the groups of drinkers in the pub had at least one person among them who had given them that special look: the one that expressed surprise and irritation that such old men had, somehow, escaped the old folks home and were on the loose in the world – in *their* space, as they would hideously express it.

'Bugger them,' Jim said; 'maybe we irritate them because we're a reminder of their mortality – in which case: good.'

'Speaking for myself, the closer I get to it – snuffing it, that is – the less it bothers me,' Winston said. 'It's dying's the problem: it might be painful. But when you're dead, why should that trouble anyone – trouble the dead one, I mean? When you're dead, you don't know it, so you can't be disappointed; or if you *do* know it, then you should be whooping with delight – if you can do that without a body.'

Big subjects characterised these lunch sessions; the old geezers did not go in for much barber shop crap – blather about the match last night, immigrants taking all the jobs, the latest Hollywood blockbusters, celebrity shenanigans, and such like.

'Indeed, old friend,' agreed Jim.

'Unless you believe all the heaven and hell tosh,' Winston continued, warming to the subject, 'which nobody really does these days, do they? And even if you believe in some sort of continued existence – disembodied or however – it can't plausibly start off with an Old Bailey trial somewhere up there in the ether; a jury, or the boss himself, examining whether you've earned eternal bliss with Mother Teresa or should be barbecued, for ever, along with Hitler, Ian Brady and the rest. Can it?'

George said: 'I've always thought an eternity of punishment a bit OTT for a loving God. It couldn't be justified even for Hitler, could it? – A few billion years, yes – for *him* – but not eternity. Perhaps God doesn't understand what eternity means because even He hasn't been around that long.'

'After you die you go to where you were before you were born: nowhere,' Winston said emphatically, blinking and tugging at his trousers' creases, and in doing so scratching the back of his hands on the underside of the vicious table top. 'No one believes he spent an eternity, either in heaven or hell, before being born. And no one feels hollow, or frightened, or disappointed, or meaningless, because he wasn't alive before, say, 1943, so why should he get upset because he won't be around after 2043? All that goes for "she" too, in case the thought police are listening.'

'I'd really miss these uplifting socials with you guys if they came to an end,' Andy said. He did not agree with Winston or George but was not able frame his reasons for the moment. Certainly not after the beers. Andy liked the idea of going on – and on, and just could not believe in his eventual termination, however strong the arguments against an after-life.

'What would a disembodied existence be like?' George asked – but of no one in particular. 'You wouldn't want food, you wouldn't want beer, you wouldn't want sex, fresh air, sleep, holidays, sunbathing, swimming, money – what would you want? And if there's nothing you want, why would you want to exist at all, in any way?'

'You're right, old friend,' Jim said. 'Old, as we are – bleedin' old – what we all regret losing, if you're at all like me, isn't the peak of brain functioning we're supposed to have had in our twenties: it's the loss of physical capacity. Isn't that right?'

He looked at his companions but no one wanted to contradict him, so he clinched the argument:

'And if it is the loss of physical capacity we regret, why should we look forwards to having *no* physical capacity, no physical existence, which is the promise of religion – all religions, I think?'

'Quite true,' Winston eagerly agreed, schadenfreude being a part of his nature, and in his case activated even by a reminder of or fresh insight into his own bleak prospects. 'It's a double whammy. When you're dead there's either nothing or there's the worst conceivable type of continued existence: as a disembodied mind.'

The Bond villain was in his element, shinning blue eyes, intimidating blinks, immaculate tailoring.

'Anyone who's woken up at two in the morning and experienced spending hours alone in the dark with his mind spinning knows what the disembodied-mind existence might be like – hell.'

'Amen to that. I should cocoa.'

'Though hell is not the word I should have chosen, I suppose.'

'You guys always such a bundle of fun?' a bleary-eyed complete stranger interrupted. He and the small group with him were standing close to the table Andy had secured, and in the noise of the pub the voices of Winston, George and the others were so raised that they would have sounded like shouting but for the general cacophony, as would everyone else's conversations. 'You're unreal – you come to pub...' He swayed. 'You come to pub t'unwind – then spend y'time talkin' 'bout how bad it's goin' be when you're dead.

'You'll find out what's in store soon 'nough anyway, won't yer, so why not jist enjoy y'drink?'

He swayed a little while delivering his quintessence of Omar Khayyam. He was a young man (of course, everybody seemed young to Jim *et al)* and the group always welcomed any unpatronising interest from young people, especially if they were female; though of course interest from a young female was unrecorded in the annals recent decades. But enjoying engagement with a youngster (anyone under fifty) did not mean that quarter would be given. Jim answered:

'If we couldn't talk about anything that just might have an unpleasant outcome, we might as well become Trappist monks. And, by the way, bad things don't get better by being ignored.'

There were two points here, but the young man – probably in his late twenties, Jim thought – responded only to the first.

'Typist monks – what ray when they're 'bout?' He'd had more to drink than the oldies and speech was becoming increasingly difficult for him, as was standing and hearing.

'It's *Trappist.* T-R-A-P-P-I-S-T, my friend,' Jim spelt out, and explained, '– the monks who don't speak unless they have to.'

Jim said no more but it passed through his mind that despite its being the information age, young people were no better informed than ever they were.

'You guys obviously – hic – not typist monks; still working are yer, or what?' the young man asked, obviously not easily put off.

The "or what?" wasn't meant to be offensive but charitably it could only mean, if the young man had thought about it: "or what the hell are you doing here at your age socialising in a City pub at lunchtime on a working day?" But he had not thought about it and Jim understood, without having to think about it himself, that the "or what?" was one of those empty locutions with which young people fill out their sentences – like "like", for example, or "kind of". As in: Do you know what? I was like kind of devastated when I like heard – if you, like, kind of know what I mean: like.

'We're not working,' Jim said with asperity, 'but we're still alive and still allowed out. It's not a social offence yet – or perhaps it is – to appear in a place of relaxation and entertainment when you're over seventy.'

'No, mate – no 'fence 'tended.' And the bleary-eyed young man looked as if he was about ready to withdraw his embassy.

'Take no notice of Jim; he's a miserable old sod, can't help it,' Andy said to the disheartened young man, and Jim dissolved in laughter as if he had received the most amusing compliment. For the moment, he delegated relations with the young and drunk to be carried on by Andy while he got on with his pint and began to wonder when the next one would arrive and who would be getting it.

He did not have to wonder for long; Ben was in need of aunty's and said, as jocularly as he could to cover his embarrassment at *having* to get up that he would "get them in" on his way back if he made it up the staircase without mishap. As soon as he was out of earshot, Jim said to George – Andy and Winston being still engaged with the young drunk: 'I suppose we should count ourselves lucky not to be in Ben's state.'

'What? – the old prostate business – yes, I suppose so, but none of us is in mint condition. It's a question at our age, Jim, of what's wrong not whether there's anything wrong. My memory's deteriorating by the day, that's for sure – frightening. And you limp. And we're all on statins or blood pressure pills or something: or on all of 'em.'

'It's funny,' Jim said, 'when I wake up in the morning and I'm just lying in bed, I feel no different from years ago. But when I go to get up – well! It's like with a second-hand car: you only find out the state it's in when you turn the engine on.'

George smiled at this and added: 'Especially in the summer, when it's warm, in the early part of the day, I can feel as good as I ever did. But you soon remember your age when the feeling wears off after an hour or so and you're clapped out. We don't have any stamina any longer at our age.'

'Yes,' Jim agreed, 'it's as though we're not only getting older but that for us the days themselves are getting shorter. If we had an active day of, say, sixteen hours when we were young, all we get now – in my case anyway – is about four or five hours.'

'How long do you think we can keep doing these booze-ups?' George asked, mostly rhetorically. 'I always wonder these days whether it's the last one; it only needs one of us to drop off the perch and they'll fizzle out, I think.'

'Maybe. There *will* be a last one, of course,' Jim answered. 'I've had a funny feeling about today's meeting since I got up. It's been going through my head since I shaved; will one of us collapse? – ambulances and all that stuff; will someone get into a fight? – Ben most likely; will one of us get mugged and beaten up; will one of us forget who he is and be found wandering in the woods in a few days' time? Will one of us simply get into a rage over the madness of things and be carried off to the funny farm gibbering?'

George said, lighting up with his Harpo grin: 'That's the going-out-with-a-bang that Winston was talking about; close as we'll get, I think.'

'We'd need to decide who's going to do what,' Jim chuckled. 'If only one of my suggestions were to happen, it would just be an embarrassment, but if all five happened on the same lunch date it would be hilarious – might even get into the papers.'

Ben had made it up the staircase and his gleaming bald head, tilted forwards, could be seen, just about, making its way through the crowd; he was focussed on his tray of drinks. The lads were all looking happier, more florid by now; Winston's face, given his basic pink and mauve complexion, was close to warning-light scarlet.

The fresh drinks arriving, an effort was made to finish what remained on the table. Then shouting was heard from behind the bar.

'What the hell's going on?' Ben asked as he banged his tray down and spilled a quarter of the drinks.

The mood of the pub had transformed; customers were soon moving rapidly towards the door.

Everyone soon understood from instructions shouted by bar staff that it was a terrorist or bomb alert. Customers were urged to leave promptly but without panic and congregate across the road.

'Bugger it, and I've just bought a round,' Ben said. 'Are we supposed to stand in the rain drinking it? Bloody ISIS.'

'Better than standing in the rain with nothing to drink,' a couple of the others said.

They took their drinks with them and rushed for the cover of an awning on the other side of the road; an awning of a women's underwear shop, as it turned out. They were blissfully unaware of the impression on passers-by that five old men, several in grubby mackintoshes, all looking at a display of bras and knickers, might make. It did not take long, however, before they turned and settled for watching the pub door, all with faces expressive and intent but only in the narrow and limited way a cat's is when the cat is waiting for its door flap to be unlocked.

A police car arrived noisily and several policemen entered the pub. Then nothing happened for a while. That was what usually happened with bomb scares and the like, and the nothing happening could go on indefinitely.

'We could just finish this one and go somewhere else,' Jim eventually suggested.

'The Nell,' George said.

'Bit of a traipse – in the rain too,' Winston said.

'We could all get in one taxi,' Andy said

'Never any around when it's raining, as you can see,' Jim said, pointing to the evident scarcity. 'And anyway, everyone standing around here is going to race for it if one does turn up. We won't get a look in.'

'Bugger it. Bugger everything. BUGGER EVERYTHING!' was Ben's contribution. 'What am I expected to do? – go into Ann Summers carrying a G and T and ask where the gents is?'

The others sympathised but not much came of it. It was mentioned that there were other pubs fairly close by; but all knew from experience that you were always spotted by the bar staff when you tried to use a pub's facilities without buying a drink. It did not matter how convincingly you appeared to search with your eyes for the friend who was supposed to be waiting for you, perhaps even taking time to glance through the menu as you strolled, apparently without hurry, to the gents.

Finishing their drinks and placing the glasses out of harm's way on the pavement under the window display, they decided to move off and have a round at what was left of the Punch Tavern in Fleet Street. They all had fond memories of the pub before it was split to make two characterless pubs, one with an entrance in St Bride's Lane; the despoliation having taken place sometime in the nineties.

They made an odd-looking party for these days, in this neck of the woods: five old, inebriated men; one limping badly; one short, fat, broken-nosed and shaven headed; one looking alternately like Bertrand Russell or Harpo Marx; one wearing trainers with blazer and flannels; and a near albino. But they were beginning to be jovial – jovial by their standards; the drink was working its magic. The shops they could see intimidated them less than usual: sushi bars, Next, GAP, Boss, Apple, Fat Face – they might even have plucked up the courage to enter one of them in their present state, just for fun.

Also, aside from the effects of alcohol, there was a change in them (it had appeared and gradually acquired distinct presence over recent years) which they all sensed in themselves and in each other, though they could not easily have described the effect of this change on their behaviour. Except, perhaps, that whenever they became aware of the change in themselves, they found it worrying and would hear a voice inside saying, *Watch it!* take care what you do, old fella.

It was, of course – the change they all felt, that is – a consequence of their age: they had all finally reached that stage of exasperation with life and their diminishing portion of it at which eccentric behaviour becomes, if not absolutely inevitable, at least increasingly likely. At the last, social conventions weaken as inhibitors. When Dylan Thomas urged the old to rage against the dying of the light, he need not have bothered. He should have sympathised instead with the standard condition of old age in which old men – it usually is old men – *do* rage against the dying of the light, as a matter of course, irrespective of poets' imperatives. Ben's recent outburst – "Bugger it. Bugger everything. BUGGER EVERYTHING!" – was a typical rage at the dying light: a younger man would have left it at "Bugger it", substituting the f word of course, even in female company; perhaps *because* in female company, for the sake of political correctness. The "BUGGER EVERYTHING" was an old man's touch of rage.

Ben tripped on something – possibly nothing of course, given he had had a lot to drink – but was caught by Jim before it got out of hand. 'Steady old-timer,' was all Jim said.

'Thanks mate – I was nearly a goner.'

At the Punch – or whatever it was called now, no one bothered to look – Winston got a round of half pints and a G and T for Ben. And Ben found aunty's while his friends, the bar being still crowded, found somewhere acceptable to stand. There must be a better pub somewhere hereabouts was the agreed view, after

49

discussing the next venue, though no one could come up with a name – anyway, pub names change.

'Running through the rain to find a pub reminds me,' Andy said, nostalgia being a prime symptom of drunkenness in the aged, 'of that time in Sligo on a Friday night when it was bucketing – when wasn't it in Sligo? – And the first two pubs we tried we couldn't even get into; they were so crowded. And it was only about 7 o'clock. What a place.'

'What I remember from Sligo,' George said, '– Christ! I do remember something, after all – was a pub with an outside aunty's, and when I went out there – it was raining heavily of course – a girl leaning on a metal barrel was throwing up all over the place. *Jesus,* I thought, watching carefully where I trod, *that's her night out over with.* But when I came back into the pub from the gents, there she was at the bar as if nothing untoward had happened, taking a swig from a fresh pint of Guinness. What a place. What a place.'

'The thing that sticks in my mind,' Jim said, 'was creepy priests all over the place. That was all before the big scandals, but the priests were in the pubs, everywhere, all smarmy and down among it – just like KGB agents would be in a Russian drinking hole, I suppose. What a place. What a place. What a place indeed. You may well ask. Christ.'

'We enjoyed it at the time though,' Andy reminded his friends. They all nodded in agreement, remembering how much more vigorous they had been even a decade ago.

Their Sligo trip was one of a series of city breaks which they started taking sometime in the nineties, always in early November. It seemed like a good idea at the time that once a year, outside the usual holiday season, they should find a European city easily accessible by Eurostar and make a long weekend of it – bit of sightseeing, visits to museums, a lot of aimless traipsing about, and a fair amount of drinking. They were great fun at first, but the ageing men eventually felt themselves too old for such capers, which had always included Tony and Bob, the friends and erstwhile workmates now dead. Sligo, Cork and Dublin were visited separately on these trips, flying from Stansted, because a former workmate lived in Sligo, his place of birth, and had returned there in his late twenties after a decade at the Minster.

Farcical things happened to the Minster lads in the various cities they visited in early Novembers. Whenever their trips were brought to mind one of them would tell, yet again, the story of Albert's hospitalisation in Bruges, or perhaps it was in Ghent – it does not matter. Albert was another former Minster employee – he ended up in Newcastle working for another insurer, but kept in touch.

'Well, my friends,' Jim began, 'at least none of us ended up in hospital in Ireland. Just imagine waking up and seeing nuns and a bleedin' priest looking down at you. It wouldn't be like that, I know; but it's the way I can't help imagining it.

'Albert was spared that. You weren't on that trip Winston,' Jim said, 'but we'd only just arrived on the train and gone straight from the hotel early afternoon for a couple of pints; that after some awful canned wine on the train; and then we went straight to a restaurant for a meal – it was early evening by then. As soon as we'd ordered food, Albert became more quiet than usual and pale: extremely pale, corpse-like. Then, when steaming plates of food were put before us, a few with that horrible strong gamey aroma, Albert rose in his place and pushed his chair over backwards and charged for the door.

'We didn't do anything immediately because we thought he was off to aunty's, but then we saw staff looking agitated and moving rapidly, one with a large plastic bucket. Next thing Albert was sitting in the lobby of the restaurant, which of course customers had to pass through, throwing up into the bucket and groaning. By the time we got to him – a couple of us – he'd decided to stand up and leave. He opened the door, took a breath of the cold fresh November air and fell – so it seemed looking from behind – flat on his face.'

'God, it was dreadful,' Ben said, meaning Albert's fall not his own lavatory experience, himself returned now from aunty's and feeling great again. The others nodded agreement and Jim continued his narrative:

'Obviously, the next thing for Albert was hospital,' Jim continued. 'We couldn't understand what was wrong because we hadn't had so much to drink during the day – yet. And we'd all had the same amount – that was the point – but he was the only one who'd fallen flat on his face.

'At the hospital, it all became clear. Albert was okay basically but had to stay in overnight for observation. He was suffering from excessive drinking. Tony had been the one to go to the hospital with him – the rest of us carried on with our meal – and he told us afterwards that when the consultant had asked Albert where he came from, and was told Newcastle, it was a moment of revelation. Then as if the vital missing clue had been uncovered, the medic let out a long "Aaaaaah!" Clearly, in his mind, if you came from Newcastle that was explanation enough for having more alcohol than blood flooding through your veins.

'Further enquiries revealed that Albert had been drinking the night before our trip, had then got to bed late, and, to cap it all, had had no breakfast in the morning prior to catching the early train for London to join us on the Eurostar.'

Andy, his complexion deteriorated by the drink, and his head looking more than ever like a pink celeriac, reminded his friends that when they had walked past the restaurant next morning traces of Albert's blood were still visible on the pavement.

'But Albert was fit enough to join us again round about lunch, wasn't he?' Ben said.

'Yes, yes – none the worse for wear,' Jim laughed, twitching his spectacles with his right hand.

'Perhaps it's true what we've always said,' Winston wondered, '– that drunks don't hurt themselves when they fall over because their muscles are relaxed. Not that I want to put it to the test.'

'I know I've had a fair amount to drink,' Ben said, changing the subject, 'this place is beginning to seem like a half decent pub.'

'We don't want to keep changing pubs every pint,' George suggested, with the extra emphasis that drunks put into their discourse.

'Wonder if the Slug and Lettuce has blown up yet,' Jim said; 'hope they change the name if it's rebuilt.' He laughed to himself.

'We'd have heard it from here,' Ben said, slurring the words slightly, 'bound t'have done.'

'Christ,' Winston said, 'we're all half blotto already and we've only had, I dunno, four or five pints is it? Pull yourselves together chaps. It's embarrassing.' The old geezers still used chaps rather than guys; their ideal world was that of *Three Men in a Boat*, a book long before their time, but that is how nostalgia often works – the longing, not unusually, is for a period preceding your own experience.

Chapter 5

They had been talking very loudly – partly because of their deficient hearing, partly because they were getting drunk, and because the pub was rowdy with other drinkers.

'If you're makin' joke abaht terrorist bomb goin' off – an' I fink y'are,' a tall pot-bellied tattooed upholder of decency interrupted, 'then yer shud be 'shamed o'yerselves. It's no laughin' matta, mate.'

He, too, was drunk, and apparently a lone drunk.

'Piss off,' the irascible Ben said loudly and with a look that gave assurance he was the man to make him if he did not.

Then, diplomatically by comparison with Ben, George said:

'We'll decide what we laugh at and what we'll be ashamed of. You, sunshine, should be ashamed of interrupting a private conversation.' He gave his opponent a moment to take it in and finished off, but under his breath:

'Why don't you find a friend to talk to – if you've got any.'

'Fuck you, you old git. I ain't deaf. Where's yer fuggin carer today, wot I'm paying good taxes for? You…'

Immediately, the lone abusive drunk found himself reeling backwards under the weight of Ben's short but round body. The lager in his half-finished pint was hurled from his glass into the air as he fell; it plashed against the wainscoting, the glass smashing when he dropped it at the moment his back collided with a tabletop. Ben had propelled himself panther-like at the torso of the pot-bellied moralist, and for a moment embraced him as he lay leaning backwards across the table's debris.

'Bloody hell – what's got into Ben, the stupid bugger?' Jim shouted. He was visibly shocked and upset. 'Is he completely off his rocker? He can get himself out of this one.'

The bar's customers, especially those sitting around the table that Ben and his prey landed on, were voluble in their advice and abuse and yelps of fear and excitement. Two men standing nearest the incident locus pitched in to pull off the raging Ben and restrain him. By now the bar staff had grasped what was going on. Three of them began pushing their way through the standing customers and weaving around tables; they had the focus and sense of purpose of a proper rescue service; from the look on their faces, they would get to the rebellious corner of their empire and restore law and order if it was the last thing they ever did. One of the young barmen had started his journey by clearing the counter in a single leap.

When they got to their objective though, the crime scene had changed materially. The tall pot-bellied one, who wore torn jeans and a grubby white tea shirt bearing the legend *Just Do It*, had exploited his weight advantage and now had Ben pinned beneath him. It was Ben whose back felt the cold slops of various beers and spirits soaking through his clothing.

Not easily fooled, they would like think, the experienced and savvy bar staff understood at once that Ben was a short, fat and elderly man in clean, smart and expensive casual wear who was being brutally abused by a yob.

The nonplussed yob offered no resistance when shown the door and told that there was no point in his returning to the pub – ever.

Order was soon restored and free replacement drinks provided to those who had had theirs spilled, and even to Ben's group, though it had suffered no loss; and the manageress made a point of apologising to Ben and expressing her hope that the unfortunate incident would not deter him or his friends from using the pub again.

'We're not used to this kind of thing happening here,' she said, 'and I'm going to make sure it doesn't happen again.'

What she had in mind she left unsaid. It crossed Jim's mind that she would institute a ban on T-shirts stamped with inane legends. And long overdue, if she does, he thought.

The old geezers had been taken aback by events and now made short work of their existing and gratis drinks, as if this might restore their calm and equilibrium. Not much was said for a few minutes. They struggled to comprehend (perhaps Ben included) what had happened and why – a brawl in a pub, involving one of their party, was something new. Entirely new.

Something wholly unwelcome too. When the power of speech returned, it was agreed to move to another venue: this place had lost whatever charm it had possessed.

Standing holding their drinks, Ben's friends felt themselves wilting under the constraint of not being able to broach the matter of his behaviour in his presence. They were in shock from what had actually happened, besides, quite naturally, feeling some terror at his apparent capacity to go berserk at the drop of a hat.

Trembling and staring through whatever was in his eyeline, Ben resembled less a pub customer than a soldier in the trenches waiting for the signal to go over the top and meet his end. He had the jitters. But like the soldier in the trenches also, his mind was occupied – seemed to be – with far away things – far away in the recesses of his mind. But what? His friends pondered the matter but to no avail. They were fretful for him – mainly for his sake, to do them justice; but they were also concerned for themselves while in his erratic company.

They did not decide where they would go before leaving the aptly once named Punch Tavern; before they did leave, Andy pointed out the appropriateness of having a punch-up in the Punch, just to relieve the tension. So the next pub was the first topic as they began listing and lurching along Fleet Street towards the Strand. A former taxi driver, Andy knew the location of several boxing halls and cheekily asked whether one of them might be Marciano's preferred choice. It was a joke that the rest were glad to see Ben took in good part. The ice still had to be broken properly, however.

'You okay after all that?' Jim asked, as they approached, haltingly, the old Reuters' premises.

It took a moment or two for Ben to understand that he had been spoken to.

'Me? Yes, I'm fine – psychopathic of course but otherwise tickety-boo. Could do with my clothes being washed and brushed, I suppose.'

An admission of psychopathy would not normally be reassuring. In this case it was. It was both a joke and evidence that Ben was aware how outrageous his behaviour had been – two good signs, and each reassuring to his friends that he could once again be conversed with as a rational being.

'We've known you were a psychopath for years, old friend, so let's put that to one side for the moment,' Jim laughed. 'But what's with the John Wayne stuff in the pub?'

'The old red mist, I suppose...'

'God, Ben–,' Jim was taken by surprise, 'we can't start getting the red mist, as you call it, every time someone speaks out of turn in a pub. We'd be fighting all the time...'

Winston interrupted, not prepared to pull any punches himself:

'Bear this in mind Ben: you're short, overweight and in your mid-seventies. You try that on a few times with blokes twice y'size and you'll know what it's like to leave a pub on a stretcher.' Winston was by now blinking furiously and strangling himself with his tie. 'And you can't expect us to pile in, as if we were all twenty-five-year-old extras in a western saloon bar fight. Anyway, you should be better at anger management than the rest of us,' Winston smiled, a joke occurring to him. 'Didn't you tell us last time that one of your daughters was an *agronomist*?'

'What?' Ben asked, utterly perplexed.

'I'll spell it out: anger management – *agro*-nomist. Geddit?'

'Christ,' Ben said, 'don't ever try stand-up.'

'But why d'you do it, Ben?' Jim asked; he simply couldn't grasp what would drive someone to – as he worded it in his own mind – such barbaric behaviour. He remembered Ben as a young man, boy really, telling him about the beautiful French girl he had recently met, and who seemed to like him; the Brigitte he soon married. Then, Ben was a happy, healthy, optimistic youngster. *God, how he's changed, poor bloke,* Jim thought, but not without reflecting that he too was much changed from the boy who loved going to scouts, had that great holiday in the west country with his friends, and so on. "And so on" – *how often we old people use this expression,* Jim thought with sadness.

'Issues at home,' Ben said, '– also, maybe, because I'm short, fat and old, as Winston so kindly mentioned. And he might have added, for that matter – ill too.'

'What issues?' Jim asked.

Fleet Street, as they lurched along it, looked unchanged despite the unkindness of the years: its demotion to a mere link road between the West End and the City.

The Telegraph and Daily Express buildings were still there, reminder of the street's former importance; and traffic and pedestrians still gave the street a deceptive air of purpose – "deceptive" because you knew that the newspaper industry had long since gone. Fleet Street had lost an industry but found no new role.

Who now occupied the former newspaper offices? Who lunched at El Vino's these days?

Winston was saddened at the vanished vitality that once extended even to side-streets, when he was young. Then, if you turned off Fleet Street, your ears would be assailed by the thunder of rolling presses preparing lies, truth, entertainment for a nation. The innumerable delivery vans that seemed to be everywhere you looked in those days were as urgent in their goal of punctual delivery as you knew their drivers were indifferent to whether it was truth or lies they carried in the back of their vans in piles of paper crudely bound tight with string. If these drivers, many of whom were politically active and staunch trade unionists, had ever been asked whether they were happy to be the magnates' messenger boys, they could only have given the old mafia excuse: it's just business.

'Why don't we stop at El Vino's?' Winston shouted to the others.

They did not all hear him – the pavements were busy and the group had become spread out. Winston shouted again and a cockney sparrow delivering something to Boots called back: 'Great idea, mate – what time?'

The others then heard Winston's repeated, lauder call – most of them – but it was not going to be easy to get a concordance.

Andy bellowed, 'Do y'remember that Mooney's further on with the really long narrow bar – that was a good pub. Still a pub, it is, I think. Or maybe it isn't. There was 'nother good Mooney's at Oxford Circus. I liked Mooney's.'

'I always liked the Blackfriars,' George yelled into the traffic.

'Yes,' Jim answered, 'and so did I, but that's in Queen Victoria bloody Street and we're half way down Fleet Street, supposed to be going to the Nell, or am I imagining that?'

'You *are* imagining it,' Winston yelled to him – Jim was ten yards ahead: 'nobody yet mentioned the Nell so far as I know, unless I had a senior moment and missed it all.'

Andy and Ben laughed, so did the others, though they did not know why; they felt they were having a good time.

This bellowed street conversation caused wry expressions on the faces of pedestrians who crossed their path, but that sort of effect was now beyond the capacity of the old men to recognise or indeed care about even if they did. They listed, lurched, and limped onwards oblivious of any censorious looks directed their way.

'Why don't we go to El Vino's?' Ben called, as if it were a fresh idea, now that he grasped what was going on. 'No one ever listens or takes notice o'my suggestions, 'course.'

'Bloody hell,' Winston said, exasperated but laughing. 'I give up. The responsibilities of leadership and all that – it's too much. Noblesse oblige ain't for me. I'm just going to keep walking until one of you pillocks twig that we should be going *somewhere.*'

'No need to get shirty, old friend,' Jim said. 'I think El Vino's is a good idea.

'EVERYONE: IT'S EL VINO'S – OKAY?' Jim shouted at the top of his voice as if inviting the whole street.

'I thought we were going to the old Blackfriars,' George said; 'now it makes sense we're walking down Flee' Street. I'm sure you mentioned Blackfriars, Jim, or someone did.'

'Christ,' was all Jim said, but he could not help laughing. It was beginning to seem like old times. And the more it did the better. He had some recollection of Ben saying something a while ago about "home" and "issues" but could not pinpoint it, and then he remembered Ben calling himself psychopathic and laughed and took out a lens wipe to clean his specs, staggering as he did so, but not feeling as much pain in his knee as usual.

'I need aunty's soon, very soon,' Ben announced, very loudly and with great determination.

He drew a peculiar look from a smartly dressed middle-aged man then crossing his path on the pavement. This man, much taken aback, must have thought for a split second that it was he who was being addressed by an aggressive, obviously inebriated person. Why should he, the innocent pedestrian must have thought, a complete stranger, be expected to know anything about the drunk's aunt? – And why would the old drunk have such urgent need of his aunty anyway? Could his aunty still be alive even? The drunk looked to be in his mid-seventies. The stranger quickened his pace – you came across some real nutters these days.

'We'll be there soon,' Winston reassured Ben. And a few seconds later: 'Here we are indeed.'

The group gathered and coalesced before making their faltering and fumbled entrance into El Vino's.

'Far be it for me to say,' said Jim as soon as they were through the door, 'but perhaps some food should be thought about – otherwise we'll be blotto before we know it.'

Winston and George agreed.

Andy could not resist saying: 'And Ben, try an' give us half an hour or so's drinking an' eating before duffing people up.'

Still in jovial mood, presumably having worked off his aggression at the Punch, Ben remembered Jim's John Wayne jibe earlier and retorted:

'The hell I will; that'll be the day,' – and all in a fair cowboy drawl. Then he disappeared to aunty's.

They were all in high spirits. A large table was found without difficulty, the busiest lunch period now over. Ben returned after a longer than usual absence, noticeably smartened up since his fight and with a fistful of paper towels in one hand; until he lost interest, he continued to dab and rub his soiled clothing with the towels.

The men looked at the menu carefully, all of them now finding it more difficult to focus, concentrate, understand, or indeed to remember what they had read even if they did manage to get a handle on the seemingly floating menu text. The choices seemed to them too sophisticated for a wine bar, but they diligently forced their eyes to focus and read the menu through despite knowing that, in the end, they would inevitably order beef sandwiches for five.

'In the old days at El Vino's,' Jim reminded them, 'it was Hobson's choice: Jacob's cream crackers and cheddar or nothing, wasn't it?'

They agreed it was, and all had fond memories of the dull staple.

'I think I'll just have a beef sandwich this time,' Andy announced to his friends, with a hint of an inflection suggesting his choice might come as a shock, certainly no inevitability.

It was a good idea, it transpired. They all fell in with it. It made things straightforward. A couple of bottles of house red were added to the order – Merlot on Winston's recommendation. They sat back and for the first time since arriving had a look about them and began to relax. Or try to relax; the memory of Ben's fracas was too fresh. But talking about something else often can take your mind off whatever is worrying you.

'One lunchtime in the old days I passed here and Denis Compton came hobbling out,' Winston said, while they waited without drink or food and tried to forget the Punch and the punch-up. Nobody responded and soon they all started looking vague, purposeless, helpless, like animals in a pen. Every time the door opened they twitched as if expecting the entry of a large man wearing a tea shirt which urged you to *Just Do It*.

The walk along Fleet Street and the present pause while waiting for food and drink had helped them sober up, get a second wind, but it also left them feeling socially uneasy, at a loss, while waiting.

Winston stuck to his memory of Denis Compton:

'He was old by then, Compton – probably he'd been meeting with whoever ghosted his articles. I say old, but he might have been younger than we are now. He was small too and limping badly; you'd never have thought he'd been a great sportsman – great cricketer.'

'People would never believe, looking at us now, that we were eligible young men once,' Jim said sullenly. 'I was anyway…not so sure about you lot.'

'Does any of it matter, though?' Ben asked, as they say, straight out of left field. 'Really matter, I mean.'

All his friends were surprised but only Jim's interest was aroused to try and find out what Ben had in mind; Andy and George began to talk cricket with Winston, now he had reminded them of the great Denis Compton.

'What do you mean?' Jim queried, very much on the watch for peculiar or potentially dangerous signs in Ben's behaviour. 'Does any of *what* matter? What are you talking about, my friend?'

'I s'pose I mean that all the things we thought were important when we were young – well, now, looking back, we don't. That's true enough, isn't it? Eligible young men – well, we might have been but so what? In the end, so what?'

The other three were now talking about how today's professional cricketers were as boorish as any other sportsmen – and, of course, other boorish sportswomen. That the old expression, "It isn't cricket", had been gutted of meaning.

'I'm *still* not sure I know what's important, as you put it, even at our age,' Jim cautiously replied to Ben. The idea interested him and after a minute or so he continued:

'I wonder if we five are representative of old people in general; I've always felt a bit of a square peg in a round hole, and I think we all have. I mean us five.'

'Go on – I can see I'm in for the ten-minute lecture, I'm all ears,' Ben said.

'None of us had a vocation for anything,' Jim began; 'we just made the best of the cards we were holding – if we did even that. That doesn't make for the happiest of lives, I think, and doesn't give you much to look back on with satisfaction in old age. So I take your point, Ben, that *it*, whatever *it* means, doesn't matter in a sense, because our lives didn't find a purpose; they were just one damn thing after another.

'And if they'd been different – say because we changed jobs or married someone else, or whatever – they'd have just been one *different* damned thing after another. And that's because we're the sort of people that we are: destined – like most other people it has to be said – to make no mark and to be disappointed in old age. For us the *it* – the meaning of our lives, if you like – had no significance, just wasn't there. We made no mark.'

Ben seemed to perk up at the thought that most people were in the same boat with him and said:

'Are most people – really, *most* of them – disappointed and unhappy in old age, do you think, Jim?'

Jim, not one to beat about the bush, said, 'We're not here to be happy – whoever said we were…? We're just here; even those individuals who do make their mark are often unhappy. Read the newspapers.'

Ben smiled and sighed deeply and looked around in search of the wine and sandwiches they had ordered, and said, laughing at the desperation of it all:

'Christ, it's a good thing you never felt a vocation for counselling. They'd have been rushing to the cliff edge like lemmings after sessions with you.'

Sandwiches and wine arrived, and eating precluded serious conversation for a time – chiefly because of the nature of the sandwiches. On this last point, there followed, eventually, some perfunctory though bitter criticism of modern restaurant, wine bar, pub presentation. Along the following lines. Why did you have to ask for English mustard – in England? How can a filled baguette be described as a sandwich? 'When you had fewer and looser teeth, or a weakly supported bridge, worse still a denture,' Andy said, 'you bloody-well knew that there was a big difference between sandwiches and baguettes.'

'The things we complain about nowadays…' George said. 'If you remember the dreadful bacon sandwiches at the Ship and Shovel off Villiers Street, with lumps of bone in the bacon that could smash your fillings when you were a newcomer and hadn't learned to expect them – that really was crap food. But we laughed it off in those days – even if we did go home with broken fillings.'

Winston, out of kilter with the mood of his friends – which was not unusual for him – said:

'These baguettes are pretty good, you've got to admit it – no argument – however bloody difficult to eat.'

He took another big bite, head on one side as he tugged violently at his so-called sandwich, like a wolf dealing with a recalcitrant part of the carcass.

Ben still had things he needed to get off his chest. What Jim had said about their lives had hit home.

'None of us is likely to divorce and never has been because it wasn't done in our day – although Winston, I know, is an exception,' Ben said. He spoke directly to Jim, assuming there was no risk of Winston overhearing. The subject was much to Jim's consternation; firstly, because Jim couldn't see how this topic was connected with what had come earlier but also, and much more, because he feared Winston might indeed overhear them. Winston was known to have a preternatural ability to hear what was outside the range of normal human hearing – or so his friends thought. For Christ's sake, Jim was saying to himself, while glaring at Ben, Winston's divorced, so bloody-well keep it down mate.

'But that's the point,' Ben continued, oblivious of Jim's facial contortions, 'he was an exception... Nowadays, everybody gets divorced at the drop of a proverbial.

'I wonder if our lives were blighted – and the wives' too of course – because we were all supposed to stick it out for the sake of the bloody children, and did for the most part. You see what I'm getting at, Jim, don't you?'

Throughout this last speech Jim had been continuing to frown and move his eyes theatrically in the direction of Winston, trying to warn Ben to keep his voice down.

'Yes, I'm keeping my voice down, aren't I?' Ben finally said quietly, getting the message and grimacing at being told off.

'Most of the couples I know in our age bracket,' Ben said, '– they're all the same: the wife ends up with nothing but contempt for the husband; the husband looks like a jailbird.'

Ben was now speaking in a confidential, almost suspicious manner. He warmed to his theme:

'I have a test of how up the creek a marriage is. When things are bad you'll find that whenever a guy is telling an anecdote in company and his missus is present, then, at a key point in the story – the point that makes the anecdote worth telling at all – the wife will interrupt and say something along the lines of, "No, Tom, that's not how it was – you've got it all wrong".'

Jim smiled and said, 'Yes, it's surprising how often that does happen.'

'And you, of course, have to say nothing afterwards about being made to look an idiot, but if you dared interrupt one of her stories with a correction, in front of *her* friends – phew, what a bollocking you'd get.'

'Of course,' Jim said, 'you realise that these days what you're saying is misogyny – misogyny most damnable. Men mustn't criticise anything about women; it's only us that have faults,' he laughed. Laughed partly at the pleasant consciousness of being in company where it was possible to speak the unspeakable and not only get away with it but find a sympathetic hearing. He and Ben were enjoying the illicit pleasure of old lags reminiscing in their own exclusive company about past break-ins, thefts, forgeries, and the like.

'Mmmm,' Ben hummed.

'Not that we men don't have faults mind,' Jim continued, keeping an eye on the others to make sure that the once divorced Winston did not hear them talking about marital relations; 'we're all flawed – men and women alike. At some level we all understand this, I think, even from an early age: we arrive screaming and fight with our siblings in the cot; we witness our parents at each other's throats; we learn of family feuds, of life-long enmities with neighbours. Then we get a glimpse of history – and what's that but a record of wars, murders, rape and pillage, greed? As Voltaire said, "A record of how, in succession, one group of people have accommodated themselves to the possessions of another group." Something like that, it was, Voltaire said, I think.'

'Still,' said Ben, agreeing mostly but probing for a weakness, 'we know all this, as you yourself say, but we carry on, often, or usually, I guess, optimistic, hopeful… Not me mind.'

'Well, we can't escape the merry-go-round, old friend, because nature plays its top trick on us, the one we call romantic love, which is only its way of ensuring that the merry-go-round keeps turning. And it always works.'

'Keep going – you're on a roll, Jim. Don't stop now.' Ben encouraged him, much amused by his old and dear friend, and proud at the same time. Heartened that Jim showed no sign of fading despite his age. None of the youngsters in here could hold a candle to Jim in this sort of discussion – Ben really believed that, though Winston and George could give him a run for his money.

Jim laughed – wild horses could not have stopped him continuing now. He was a far cry from the irritable old man who had walked under Holborn Viaduct and down Farringdon Street earlier in the day twitching his shoulders angrily at this and that intolerable aspect of modernity. All it took to change him – aside from the beer – was having someone to talk to; someone, that is, who listened with genuine interest while you talked. Jim knew the difference between genuine interest (as all old people do) and the simulated overdone interest that well-meaning people give to the game old codgers still willing to have a go, and which social workers presumably are trained to provide. Fake interest, as Mr Trump might describe it, and he should know. Jim smiled to himself as it struck him that Trump was of an age he must have experienced a fair amount himself.

They are not that easy to find, these genuine listeners, when you are over seventy – as all five friends knew – particularly so if you have got something interesting or controversial to say. It is as if society deems it unseemly to be feisty, to hold strong opinions and fight for them, after you reach a certain age – unless you are a celebrity of course. The old, it seems, should be passive; there, alive, solely to be condescended to; to be dealt with patiently, as children are dealt with. The old are merely an opportunity to bring out the best in younger people – certainly no longer serious players in the active adult world. But not Jim though, or his friends, exceptions each of them, for better or worse.

He carried on now where he left off, looking increasingly merely sixtyish as he warmed to his theme:

'Love. Love. It's the cruel delusion that makes us believe – sadly for only a short time – that one woman or one man is significantly different from all the others. Then, when the painted veil is lifted on this delusion, if we're unlucky we find that we're married and there isn't even the compensation of friendship remaining. But that's a compensation devoutly to be wished, old friend. If you emerge from love to find you have friendship, you've hit the jackpot.

'It's been said often enough before…'

Andy just picked up on the phrase and instantly broke off from his cricket debate to interject:

'But that's not going to stop you from saying it all over again if I know you, Jim.'

'Bugger off!' Jim replied good humouredly, otherwise continuing his discourse without hesitation:

'…but given the general propensity for people to fall out with one another you should never get married while still in love. Never, that is, when your judgement is in suspension. Just have your affair, and when the flames burnt out, if affection and friendship and common or compatible interests survive…well, obviously, that's the time to think about marriage. The marriage of true minds. I've been lucky: I, or *we* I should say, Maureen and me, married blind, but fortunately we did find friendship after the veil was lifted. It doesn't happen too often though. Of course, there's no point giving this advice to young people – or old ones, for that matter – because the deluded state is pretty-well proof against outside influences, good or bad.'

'You can't half talk, Jim – you always could. You're my hero.'

'Look at any David Attenborough telly series, whether about insects, animals, birds or sea life, and what will it tell you about relations between the sexes? If the male isn't needed after procreation, nature programmes him to die, or simply to wander off – at worst he becomes a meal for his partner.

'There *are* examples of life-long partnering in the animal world, but so many instances in nature of male redundancy *after* the act ought to make us cautious about what to expect from the human male and female relationship.'

'This is why I'd miss these lunches, Jim, being able to talk freely. Even to talk codswallop freely – it's a tonic or something. You know what I mean.'

'I do, Ben. And I need more of your tonic than most,' Jim agreed.

'You know all those pages in the papers and mags – advice on sex problems?'

'Yes, what about them? It's late in the day for you to bother about problems in bed, isn't it?' Jim asked with wry smile, a bit fearful of what might be coming.

'I mention it because they miss the point – those articles do, I mean. All the nonsense about how he wants it when I don't, or he likes what I hate. What's really wrong, always, is that there's no meeting of minds. That's what I think. People have lost or never had the ability to explain themselves to each other and get a sympathetic hearing. Or should I say empathetic? The word empathy – that's the one that's on everyone's lips these days, though no one ever used it when we were young. It's on people's lips because there's none of it about, bloody hell. When it's there, you don't have to keep yapping about it, and you don't have problems in bed. When there ain't no *empathy*, you might as well be having sex with a prostitute.

'When I look back on things…the best of it was those times when I was in tune with Brigitte. In tune sounds corny. Each of us knew what the other was thinking, not merely understood each other when we talked. Though we did talk then – properly. That's what I look back on nostalgically, wishing it could come back, not the other stuff. It lasted a few years. Now I only have that with you Jim, and with the others to some extent.'

'I hope it doesn't mean you want to go to bed with *us* now, old friend,' Jim joked, beaming with Pickwickian benevolence.

'Seriously, if you snuffed it – it sounds absurd, I know – but I reckon I'd have had enough too, mate. Nobody left on my wavelength.'

'All for one and one for all, hey,' said Jim. It was all he could think of in reply. It didn't quite suit, but he was disconcerted, touched by what his old friend had said and somewhat lost for words altogether. Lost for words! – He realised it was absurd in the context of their discussion about talking.

'Test cricket's had it,' George was saying to Winston and Andy, the erstwhile taxi driver beginning to look tired and greyish, either from illness or because he was bored stiff: 'a game that lasts for five days in an age when people can't concentrate on anything for more than five minutes. The few who still go to the matches – Christ, even they can only stick it by getting totally drunk and staying that way until it's all over and inevitably the Aussies have won again. The so-called Barmy Army.'

Winston and Andy did not argue; they did not disagree; in Andy's case, he wasn't interested one way or the other. Anyway, of course things in general were not as good as they used to be, and that must include cricket.

Jim and Ben had come to a kind of dead end, and both were at a loss for a new line of conversation. Neither felt like joining or prolonging the cricket debate.

The second bottle of merlot was addressed. As Jim took a sip and sighed deeply, and gazed aimlessly about him, he noticed a young couple sitting alone in a corner – they were, he judged, in their mid-twenties. They were not staring moonstruck into one another's eyes; they were having a lively conversation, one which caused them to laugh frequently. They were also eating steak and chips, but not with any evident interest in the food; it was eating to justify occupying a table. Jim could see that when their eyes did make contact from time to time, their faces glowing with youthful vitality, it was in an avid and soul-searching way, and they were delighted with what they saw in each other, joyful in their good fortune, and they laughed all the more – at nothing, Jim was sure, other than their good fortune. Their eyes met for brief moments only, the experience too intense to sustain for longer. Jim remembered what it was like.

Jim realised he was happy in the unalloyed happiness he could see; after all, he had had his own brief experiences of the great delusion – of splendour in the grass – a phrase he was now mouthing silently to himself, moist-eyed and in a near swoon of nostalgia.

A host of memories came surging. He would have been irritable had anyone spoken to him, brought him back to the now. The sense of being back in his youth was so strong upon him, and so welcome. He felt again with all the force as when it happened fifty years ago – yes, it must be fifty years – he felt again the frightening pulse of life that exploded through him when he had taken hold impulsively of his girlfriend's warm and willing hand in a cinema in Cornwall, in a town he could not possibly remember now. *I damn near jumped out of my seat then,* he thought, and smiled about. 'How mad and bad and sad it was, but then how it was sweet, according to the poet: but it wasn't mad or bad or sad,' Jim said to himself, 'only sweet, very sweet, a sweet without which life would not have been worth it.'

Jim then strangely experienced the word "sweet" guiltily, as if it was a profanation in the mind, let alone the mouth, of an old man like himself. He tried to imagine his friends mouthing, uttering the word sweet and it did not seem right, even if he thought of them describing their grandchildren. A word for the young, he thought; what has sweetness to do with old age, decrepitude, wrinkles, smells, buggered-up knees, decay in all its glory?

Ben decided it was time for a visit to aunty's, and when he was out of sight, the others looked quizzically at Jim, wanting his opinion on Ben.

'He's okay now, I think. He's depressed about home life, poor chap, and he's not well, is he?' Jim answered their unspoken enquiry. 'Probably worse than he's letting on.'

'But we can't have him going off the handle again, can we?' said Winston.

'No.'

'Mmmmm.'

They thought quietly about the matter for a couple of minutes.

'Here he comes, shush.'

'That was a quick one.'

'And he's not dragging a body behind him,' said Andy. 'So no fight in the lavatory – unless he's left the body in a cubicle.'

'Shush.'

Chapter 6

Remembering the long ago in a cinema in Cornwall had led Jim to recall another time in the West Country – a week's holiday which he took with Winston and George a year or two after his cinema epiphany. *Those earlier selves*, he thought – *Winston, George, and himself – might have been different people from those now sitting in El Vino's; and so they were*, he was sure. But it was good to summon up the memories.

In the nineteen sixties a holiday for most people living in the London area still meant going somewhere in Britain, usually somewhere in England. Jim and his friends, who were all still working at the Minster at the time, got the idea of hiring a car and driving to Cornwall for a week; none of them owned a car though they had all passed the test and would share the driving. In Cornwall, and perhaps on the way through Devon they would take up bed and breakfast options to fit in with plans made on the hoof. No one wanted to map anything out in advance; it would be more of an adventure, more fun to see what came up.

George took it upon himself to sort out the car hire. Then, on a Saturday morning in mid-July at around ten o'clock, the weather sunny and warm, the three of them met at a garage in Whitechapel to pick up their Ford Anglia. Whenever George recalled that Ford over the years, he thought that when people say, as they do in every generation, that things are not as well made as they used to be, there is certainly one big exception: cars. The cars of the nineteen sixties were crap; he knew that from experience, and he was sure his friends would agree. In the sixties, though, any car that more or less worked and could take you all over southern England, seemed like a piece of magic.

When they got on the North Circular that Saturday morning, which was not necessarily the straightforward start for a journey to Cornwall from where they had begun, they were in great high spirits. All three had the mops of hair fashionable at the time; Jim's was an unkempt stack of brown that would have been straight if ever combed; Winston had a wavy pile of light blond hair as an ideal background to his piercing blue eyes and clear light skin; George's mop was an indeterminate darkish brown or brownish black. They were all wearing open-necked shirts, sports jackets, and trousers with smart creases in them, and brown shoes to signal they were on hols and free of their worn-down black work shoes. They were slim, lithe, strong and happy young men – of the lucky generation that escaped both war and national service. Their only regret, if you had asked them at the time, was that they were always short of cash.

They were outside and west of London, Jim remembered, before they had their first argument. George said:

'Where are we going to have our first stop? Or when, maybe?'

'We've only been driving for an hour; it's a long way to Cornwall,' Winston answered. (It had been Winston doing the first shift as driver and he was enjoying it.)

'Well, when do you intend a stop? Or are you just going on until you've had enough? Don't we get any say?'

Jim said: 'Now, now, girls – no squabbling. Next you'll be asking, "When is it my turn?"'

'Are we nearly there yet?' said Winston in a five-year-old's squeaky whine.

George ignored him and asked Jim if he could look at the South England map that was on his lap.

'Careful.' Jim said, passing the map back to George, who was in the rear along with some of the excess luggage. 'It's been folded so many times now, it's falling apart; my dad's had it for years, so it's completely out of date anyway.'

Before the hand-over was completed, a large square of paper from the disintegrating map – that part bearing the representation of the area of southern England and its coast line which included some famous resorts: Eastbourne, Brighton, Bognor Regis, etc. – detached itself and took erratic flight out of the nearside rear window. All the windows had been wound down at the start of the journey. There was no air conditioning in the car nor ever the remotest expectation that there might be or should be.

The three of them roared with laughter and George, pointing, shouted, 'That's Brighton floating away down there.' And then they began to laugh uncontrollably. They were hysterical; the holiday had really begun; this was how it was supposed to be.

The rest of the day went like a dream. They took a side road early in the afternoon intending to find a field to pee in unobserved; afterwards, they had trouble locating the main road again and eventually stopped when they came to what struck them as a beautiful English market town. They had lunch, quite late, in an ancient pub – low ceiling, exposed beams, inglenook fireplace, yokels in the corner: all they could have wished for. It was only when they were back on the road and miles away that it struck George, who was now driving: 'What was that place called – where we had lunch?'

'No idea,' said Winston and Jim simultaneously, and they all laughed again. The feeling of freedom – no Minster, no parents, driving with no fixed objective – it was as intoxicating as the beer. Almost.

Of that first day of their Odyssey, what stuck in the minds of the three lads, apart from the fun of the journey and the driving itself, was their first bed and breakfast experience. They often reminded one another of this experience down the years.

They found an attractive little town (chiefly what made a little town attractive was its supply of decent looking pubs) and after searching a few back streets they found a terraced two-storey house, not posh, advertising B&B at a cheap price. They gathered at the door and pressed the bell but heard no sound. After several goes at pressing the unresponsive bell and waiting a minute or two, Winston decided to use the knocker, a heavy iron object that looked as if it had been painted innumerable times but without anyone ever removing the flaking rust first. Winston made the mistake of lifting the knocker up to a ninety degrees-to-the-door angle, and when he let go, not only the door but the house seemed to shake.

'Blimey!' George said, and it was touch and go whether they waited or ran off like naughty children. Before the door opened they heard a dull slow heavy booming tread coming towards them from behind the door. When the footsteps ceased and the door creaked open they half expected to be confronted by Boris Karloff. Instead, there stood, swaying slightly, a vague-faced but tall and heavy old lady who had considerable wrappings of towelling around her lower legs.

The old lady was first to speak:

'It's the dropsy, you know. But you be young men and wouldn't know anythin' 'bout that, I dare say.'

The lads were secretly looking at each other half anxious and half amused, and all wondering if the best thing would be to apologise for calling at the wrong house. Or, again, just run off like children.

'I can take the three of yer but only one night mind. You'll only need one room, that-un at the front with three beds. Get yerselves inside with yer bags, then, and I'll introduce yer to Isiah himself. He be in the parlour, as he have been, an' no trouble mark, these past ten years. Don't be bustlin' round him too lively like or he'll flip most probable, if yer do.'

While the lads were stacking their bags in the hall, Jim managed to say a word out of earshot of Mrs Beamish, she having just told them that was her name but that she couldn't help still thinking of herself as a Drayton, to which Winston had mischievously replied, 'No, of course not.'

Jim's word was three: 'What a laugh!'

George whispered, while they stood waiting awkwardly for further instruction, 'We'd better check there's no open coffin in the basement before risking any shut-eye. If I hear an organ playing in the night, I'm off – even in me jimjams.'

From the landing, Mrs Beamish called for them to bring their bags upstairs and she would show them their room.

'I 'ope yer like the room, now it's decorated like. Meself, I can't help still seein' it as it was when my Drayton, bless his soul, died 'ere of the fever. But that's all past an' you don't want a be hearin' such like, I dare say.

'For a wash yer goes down an' out back. There's a room at back o scullery – all mod cons – yer just 'ave to 'ope it's not rainin' when yer need it. Yer put a shillin' in t'make it work.

'Well, that's it boys, I dare say… When yer ready to, come down an' knock on the parlour door – not too loud, mind – an' we'll see what Isiah thinks of yer. Oh, an' will yer be wantin' a dinner? – there's some rabbit shot t'other day.'

'No!'

'No, thanks.'

'No, thanks very much. We're meeting someone.'

'So long as you're back by ten o'clock. It's locked up then.'

'Thanks, Mrs Beamish,' said Jim. The lads needed time alone to plot their escape.

'Oh, and there's a full breakfast at eight o'clock – opposite the parlour. No one else here presently, so you'll be comfy.'

'Thanks.'

'Thanks.'

'Thanks, very much.'

They faced up to their obligations and after a short time went downstairs to the parlour, butterflies in their stomachs, and each glad that he had the others with him to face the unknown. At the parlour door, George looked at Winston and Winston looked at George, and Jim, exasperated, said, 'Oh, for God's sake!' and made as if to bang on the door and show them how it was done. But he was forestalled; the door moved away from his fist as Mrs Beamish opened it from the inside and beckoned.

'Ah! I thought I 'eard yer. Come in; Isiah's had his night-time sedatives. He likes to see everyone who comes to stay; it makes him feel he be still part of the business.'

The boys moved gingerly into the over-furnished room. They immediately saw that the so-called parlour doubled as a furniture store – or museum; it had about ten easy chairs, and each of them both unique and ancient. They also saw that Isiah was at present sitting in the middle of the room facing to the far side that they were not in. He was in a high-backed chair and all they could see was the top of his large, bald head.

Mrs Beamish signalled, using violent hand gestures, that the reluctant young men should move across the room to a position facing Isiah. In the end, however, because they hardly moved, Mrs Beamish gave up the semaphore and went behind the boys; from there she spread out her arms and herded her reluctant guests into place, all rather as a sheep dog would have dealt with recalcitrant sheep.

Jim, Winston, and George could see, now they were in front of him, that Isiah watched the passing scene with his right eye only – in fact, only the right side of his face worked, and that not well. That he had suffered a stroke was obvious, but how much his mind was affected, if at all, they could not know or even guess from merely staring at him.

'Say hello to him and ask if he's feeling better,' Mrs Beamish instructed.

They all obeyed and said, 'Hello, Mr Beamish – Isiah, sir.' And from nerves Winston blinked frequently in his disconcerting way.

'Are you feeling better, sir?' Jim shouted at Isiah, assuming he must be deafish.

Mr Beamish made some gurgling noises, dribbled from the left side of his mouth and twitched his right shoulder, whereupon Mrs Beamish jumped to his side and put her ear to his mouth. After a minute, she divined that he was spooked by Winston's blink. The guests were relieved of their obligation, by a wave of Mrs Beamish's hand, and without further ado hit the town for the night. They had no time to lose as any festivities would have to end before the Angelus for lock up at the Beamish B & B at ten o'clock.

The pub, the first they came to, did not disappoint; it was crowded and jolly with normal people intent only on feeling happier by the end of the evening than they were at its beginning.

All the experiences of that first day were ever after remembered by the three men with fondness and amusement, except for something George had said when they entered the pub and saw what they took to be a young West Indian serving behind the bar.

'Blimey, they're everywhere now – even in darkest West Country,' said George.

'Yep,' said the other two.

And then they ordered drinks and got on with their evening's entertainment.

Whenever George remembered himself in that pub on that night and what he had said, he winced: it was a remark that would be inexcusable today. But he knew that in the sixties most other white English people might have said the same thing without feeling embarrassed and while still believing themselves to be decent people, and even liberal lefties. It was the wrong attitude, George once said to Jim when they had been reminiscing about their holiday, but they simply could not see it at the time, could they?

'No,' said Jim, 'we couldn't.'

'I don't think I said it in a hostile way,'

'Every age is criticised by its successor, I suppose,' said Jim. 'I mean, for example, at the beginning of the twentieth century, most men, including many of the most intelligent –'

'And women, don't forget,' grinned George.

'You haven't heard my example: most *men* sincerely thought it would be wrong to give *women* the vote. Joking apart, we can't imagine how they could think like that, but go back another century and our ancestors saw nothing wrong in buying black people in Africa and transporting them across the Atlantic to be sold as slaves.'

'Lots of our beliefs, from when we were young, are unacceptable today,' said George, 'on the death penalty, on sex outside marriage, for God's sake! – We would have liked it, sex, that is, if we'd got the chance, but we would have thought it wrong probably. Then there's the question of gay relationships, equal pay for men and women – and loads of other things.'

Jim, thinking carefully about it beforehand, had said, 'Judging the past by the standards of today is a tricky business. Some things that happened in the past – like, say, the holocaust or slavery – obviously can't be forgiven or excused simply by saying that attitudes have changed. Other things, like our old view of gender equality and sex outside marriage are embarrassing to think about now but forgivable – more or less forgivable, I think, because of the way we were brought up. I think so anyway, me old mate. We believed what we were told – as most people always do. We were brainwashed. Think of all those films set in Africa starring Stewart Granger or Clark Gable as the jungle guide: the blacks carried the supplies and at the first sight of a lion we'd be shown them running off in panic and Gable standing firm to tackle the beast.'

'He had the rifle.'

'Exactly. But some of our other beliefs in those days, well, they're unfashionable now but not necessarily wrong. And I haven't given them up in fact, and I don't think I could be persuaded to.'

'Such as?'

This was the type of conversation Jim loved:

'Oh, today they say socialism or communism is discredited and dead; I just don't believe it, as Victor Meldrew would say. It's only dormant, in my opinion, and will be back sooner rather than later. And current beliefs about smacking children: violence breeds violence, the so-called experts tell us, but we've not been smacking children for decades now and what's the result? The result is much more violence from children, including routine possession of knives among schoolchildren in London and elsewhere. And all the guff we're fed about pop music – what great artists many of the musicians are, and how immortal their music is: that's all crap in my opinion. And you know, must remember I'm sure, that I thought exactly that even when I was young. When the sixties generation disappears up the crematorium chimney, no one will listen to the Beatles anymore – few do now, I suspect, and of them almost no youngsters, I bet. Pretty soon all those famous sixties pop groups will be as dead as Donald Peers.'

'Who?'

'Exactly.'

'Jim, you're an old fogey now, no argument about that, but fifty years ago you were a young fogey. You've just proved that.'

After another pause for serious thought, Jim said: 'What should make us despair is the thought that perhaps everything we believe now, even now when we're on the brink – all the latest right-on, bang up to date ideas (if only we were bang up to date, you'll say), it'll all likely be looked back on in fifty years' time as wrong, muddle-headed, whatever. God moves in mysterious ways.'

'Makes you wonder why we bother,' George said, and that had been the end of that colloquy.

When the three of them got back to the B&B that first night of their holiday, at a quarter to ten, the door was unlocked and they hurried up to their room. Their sleep was deep and untroubled. In the breakfast room next morning they found one of the three tables, a round one, laid for a meal, and there was a promising smell of bacon coming from the passage. The table already had various cereal boxes on it and a huge jug of milk. They sat down pleasantly surprised and then Mrs Beamish appeared – literally appeared – she had been on her knees polishing the floor and hidden by a table.

'Have your cereal now and I'll bring the tea and hot stuff in a few minutes,' she told them.

It proved to be a gargantuan hot breakfast including eggs, bacon, sausage, fried bread, kidneys and grilled tomatoes; and Jim, Winston, and George saw that they were expected to eat it all, for Mrs Beamish took time off from polishing to sit and watch them at it. They did not disappoint her. It passed through the minds of Mrs Beamish's young guests, while they ate, that if they were ever this way again then this was the place for a breakfast. They even got a smile from their host when she saw empty plates. The sting in the tail was her then announcing that when they were ready to leave they should come down and settle up and say goodbye to Isiah – he particularly wanted to see them off.

In the parlour and facing Isiah, the lads were told by Mrs Beamish that Isiah had said that he liked them very much and that they reminded him of mates he had had in the 8th Army when they had been fighting Rommel together. And he hoped he had not frightened them too much the previous night. He just wanted to shake their hands, wish them well, and warn them of the dangers of swimming in the sea – which last warning Mrs Beamish took care to give them now in front of Isiah.

Mrs Beamish then told the lads to shake Isiah's right hand, but not too hard.

Winston was first, then George, and then Jim. They all said something banal, such as, 'Nice to have met you, Mr Beamish.' And the working eye and side of Isiah's face was evidently moved, in both senses.

Then Winston noticed Jim look towards the window in what he at first thought was an ill-mannered indifference to Mr Beamish, and he was about to reprimand him when he realised that tears were freely rolling down his friend's cheeks. He felt stirred himself, unusual for him, and he could see, now that he looked, that George's eyes were glistening. *Christ. Best not to notice,* he thought, which was unusually sensitive for Winston.

Whenever the three friends got together again over the years and the events of this holiday were recollected and talked about, Jim's tears were never mentioned, nor was any reference made to the emotional state of all the young men on parting with Mr Beamish – except for an occasional: He wasn't a bad old stick, was he?

Isiah and his wife for ever remained vivid in the memories of each one of the lads. Did anyone else remember them?

Chapter 7

There had been a lull in the conversation at El Vino's following Ben's return from aunty's – no attempt at a fresh topic had taken hold – and the old men were beginning to feel jaded again. If they had been at home they would have let their heads fall back and had a snooze in an armchair. It was Andy who made the effort and roused the others:

'More wine, or more sandwiches, or both – what'll it be? Decisions, decisions? Or should we pick a fight with one of the other customers?'

'Christ, give it a rest, Andy, or it'll be you who gets the bunch of fives,' Ben replied, half irritated, thank goodness half amused also.

Winston blinked, looked slightly sinister, and all the more handsome for it – a blond/albino Christopher Lee; he adjusted his trousers to ease their tautness over his knees, and said: 'Remember *Key Largo* when the gangster, who of course was played by Edward G Robinson, is asked what he wants out of life, and he replies: "More, I want more," with an insane gleam in his eye?'

'Yes,' said George eagerly, 'I *do* remember: Bogart was the hero but it wasn't he who asked, was it? It was Barrymore, the guy in the wheelchair, I think.'

'And did Bogart or Edward G or Barrymore have more sandwiches, or wine, or both?' Andy interrupted.

Jim said, 'I'm not sure it didn't end up with your third option, Andy – the fight, and Barrymore's wheelchair being overturned!'

There was mild interest and amusement over this exchange, excepting Andy, who didn't throw his hands up in despair but obtained relief from uttering a string of expletives, all, as they say, under his breath, while mopping his brow with a tissue.

A portly waitress of middle age, not the one who served them when they arrived, extrovert in appearance – overdone makeup, etc. – looked at their table as she passed. Her whole demeanour proclaimed that she enjoyed her work and life in general.

'Anything I can get you handsome young gentlemen? I s'pose it's a stag do, is it? Which one of you's getting married then?' She said all this in a powerful contralto, and rounded it off with a peel of laughter like the clanging of bells.

Andy liked her immediately and entered into the banter enthusiastically:

'El Vino's is the last place you expect to fall victim of sexual harassment,' a mock look of distain on his face, a face which more than ever looked as if it had recently taken a hit of grapeshot at point-blank range. 'Keep it up though, we're not ones to complain. We understand how difficult it must be for females to control their emotions in the presence of five hunks in their prime.'

'Gawd,' said the waitress, 'I shouldn't of started nothin' with you lot, should I? What's *your* name then – Percy Prong?

'Anyway, *do* you want anythin', my luvs? An' no backchat mind – you know what I mean by anythin': keep it clean.'

Their mood much lifted by the waitress' friendly humour, they exuberantly ordered more wine and a selection of cheeses with bread and biscuits.

While they were waiting, Ben said, 'She's a breath of fresh air, isn't she?'

Jim agreed:

'She is, indeed, and we didn't have to put up with her assuring us it was all "no worries" and telling us to have a nice day. But I wonder, though, if she's got a miserable old bastard like us at home. It's hard to believe she has.'

'You mean like my trouble and strife has,' said Ben.

'No,' said Jim, somewhat disingenuously. 'I was thinking about all our wives having to put up with all of us. They have a point of view too, you know.'

'Our wives are just like her, I bet, when we're out of the way,' Andy said.

'Absence makes the wife grow happier,' said Winston.

Jim, unable to restrain his tendency to lecture at the drop of a hat, intending his words for Ben but generalising because everyone was listening, said:

'What husbands and wives need is to be a bit more forgiving of each other. How can you live with someone for years, decades even, and not offend them, whether it's by accident or because you simply have to blow off steam now and then? If you can't be forgiven, or you can't forgive your other half, then the game's not worth the candle. The church has got one thing right: forgiveness ought always to be on the table. To be there for the repentant, as they would say.'

'Great speech,' Winston said, conveying that it was just that, in his opinion – speech, words. 'We're all in favour of forgiveness – all in favour until we have something to forgive. Or someone.'

Wine and cheese soon arrived. 'Here we are, my dears,' said their ideal waitress. 'Tuck in and don't forget to eat while you're drinking – not if you want to avoid the milk of magnesia later. That's how it always ends up with my hubby, though, bless him.' Then, before leaving her lads to get on with it, she hesitated, before asking Andy, quietly for her: 'Who's the one who looks like the James Bond baddy?' and she nodded towards Winston to make clear who it was she had in mind. Flattered because he had of course heard, Winston adjusted his tie, assumed an expression even more minatory than his usual one, and said, 'Take care, Miss Galore: in describing me as looking like the baddy, you risk a sticky end, as they say.'

'Oooooh, promises!' she replied, and was quickly off to banter elsewhere.

'This is all we've got to look forward to now, I suppose,' George said, as they all watched her deftly make her way around the tables without buffeting any of the customers. 'This is as good as it gets.'

'Yes,' Andy said, 'talk, innuendo, but no action – no action in any sense.'

'Well,' Jim said, 'that's how it's been for most of our lives, hasn't it – not just since we got old?'

'Here we go again. You've wound him up and he's off at a canter,' Winston said.

'As Andy says,' Jim continued unperturbed, 'little or no action in any sense of the word. A life in motor insurance couldn't by any stretch of the imagination be described as a life of action, but we took to it – some of us anyway – like ducks to water. And as for the other "action" – well, we like to think we had our moments but the truth is we married after scant experience and then, meekly submitting to the prevailing expectations of the time, in due course contributed our little bit to the nuclear family ideal.'

'And much bleedin' satisfaction did it give us, or to the said nuclear family, or to society, or to Uncle Tom Cobley,' said Ben.

The old geezers laughed hollowly and were suddenly in sombre mood again, something which easily happened nowadays – another symptom of their age.

'A book of verse, a flask of wine, a plate of cheese, and Ben beside me, moaning in the wilderness,' intoned Jim, thespian-like, while cutting himself a greedily large portion of cheddar, a portion he could only have justified had he been told by at least three of his friends that they would not be wanting any.

Ignoring Jim's Omar Khayyam adaptation, George said:

'I suppose every generation of old men has looked back in disappointment, like us…'

'Bloody-well hope so,' Ben interrupted. 'P'raps the only reason the young don't look back in disappointment is because they don't have any "back" to look at.'

'That's a good one for you, Ben,' Winston said. 'Not many previous generations lived this long,' he continued. 'The sociologists would say that ours is a problem of success, I suppose, though success depends on your point of view, as we all know. It doesn't feel like it from where I'm sitting, that's for sure.'

George said: 'Why we should be thought lucky simply because many of us live long enough to experience life in an old people's home – well, I just don't get it.' This was said with feeling and perhaps even a touch of anger. Some of the feeling, however, was coming from the alcohol, which was beginning to get to him again – indeed to all of them – as it does.

Andy had been trying to cut himself a piece of Manchego while George was speaking, but he was having to overstretch the table to do it. It became almost a minor disaster. Because the

Manchego was extremely hard he had to exert maximum pressure on his knife. He succeeded in cutting through the cheese – beads of sweat accumulating over his brow – but the force of the final breakthrough projected his portion into the air with a velocity that made it look probable, for an instant, it might reach another table before touching down.

In the event, it landed on the carpet without causing inconvenience to other customers.

The cheese incident caused unwonted laughter from Andy's friends and triggered a string of unfunny, alcohol-fuelled witticisms such as 'hard cheese, old boy', 'don't get cheesed off about it, mate', and 'I had that cheese in the back of a cab once'.

'Hilarious, yes, but don't bust a gut over it,' Andy irritably responded.

'And, incidentally – you lot – me being a taxi driver since I was twenty-five, I think I *did* see a fair amount of life in my working days, contrary to what Jim says – more than if I'd stayed doing insurance, that's for sure. Did I ever tell you…?'

'Yes,' they all yelled at him. 'Yes, not again, please!'

Andy had left motor insurance behind him in his mid-twenties, partly because he was discontented with it – how could any young person not be at least partly discontented with the prospect of a career in insurance? – And partly because one of his uncles was a London taxi driver; Uncle Jack had encouraged the career change and helped Andy master the Knowledge.

He never regretted the move. He enjoyed the feeling of being his own boss from an early age, the excitement of working nights rather than a day shift if he felt disposed to, the tips, regularly visiting interesting places such as airports, theatres, nightclubs; most of all, he got a buzz from carrying famous people in his cab, an occasional but always welcome experience. "Celebrities" they were called now. He had ferried his share of celebrity sportsmen and women in his cab, politicians too, and actors, comics, military figures, John Betjeman once, an Archbishop. He could tell stories about the meanness or generosity of film stars – or of how ordinary they looked and indeed were, met face to face.

Thoughts of how he had begun his career as a cab driver – terrifying at the start of his first day, when he felt he could not remember the location of anywhere in London – these memories always brought him back to thoughts of his childhood home in Shernhall Street in Walthamstow. He had been born in the three-bedroom (though it only just scraped through on that description) end of terrace house in Shernhall Street, and didn't move out until he got married in the church a couple of hundred yards away on the other side of his street.

But how basic and poverty-stricken his childhood looked to him in retrospect; he could not remember there being a fridge when he lived in his first and only family home, though by the time he married presumably one had been acquired; there was no television; the floors in the two small living rooms – one for meals and sitting in to listen to the radio, the other for best – were covered in linoleum but had no carpets; there was no central heating, only fire places which belched smoke if the coal was lit. The house had been built without bathrooms but a jerry-built, unheated facility had been added in the late fifties to the back of the kitchen, itself a tiny room with little space for anything other than its sink (cold water only) and gas cooker.

If he made the effort, Andy could remember vividly the day an Ascot was installed (*late fifties again,* he thought) and hot water became available at the flick of a switch. It must have been a great event because Andy was sure he could accurately picture to himself the two men who installed it – wearing their oldest three-piece suits, collarless shirts and flat caps; oh, and fags constantly hanging from the sides of their mouths, the ash always falling unconsidered straight to the floor to be trodden into the linoleum. They would have been men in their thirties. Andy mentally allowed for the tendency for men in those days to look at least a decade older than men of a similar age today.

An abiding memory of Andy's was of his dad and him sitting in the all-purpose living room, on opposite sides of the fireplace, in simple armchairs with wooden armrests (under the cushions of which old newspapers were stored for reasons never explained). His dad was alert, unmoving and holding a poker aloft, and the young Andy, similarly alert and quiet, was waiting. What they were both waiting for was the appearance of mice. There were always mice and if you kept quiet enough for long enough they would emerge and give you an opportunity to take them out with an accurate whack with the poker. Perhaps the prevalence of mice owed something to the floors never being quite free of crumbs; there was never a vacuum cleaner and the broom always left a little for the rodent guests.

'Don't move or say anyfink,' his dad whispered, 'there's one on your right, by the side o'y'chair.'

The mouse heard the whisper and froze.

'Keep still, son, I'm goin' to 'ave a go at the bleeder.'

Andy remembered that he was still wearing short trousers at the time and his bare legs had made him feel particularly vulnerable.

'Gertcher!' his dad said as he leapt towards Andy's chair brandishing his poker, bringing it down with utmost violence on the linoleum under the chair. He fell and put another gash in the already much damaged floor covering. He had missed the mouse. The instant his failure was apparent to him and he saw the mouse scamper off, he shouted: 'Andy, stamp on 'im – stamp on 'im!'

The mouse had run to the middle of the floor and then frozen in fear as it became aware of Andy's mum entering from the kitchen. Dad had shouted his 'stamp on 'im' from his position on all fours by Andy's chair. His son was his last hope in this particular battle of the ongoing war, but Andy was too squeamish to attempt, or even pretend to attempt, to stamp on the attractive little creature. By the time his dad was on his feet again and back in the battle, the mouse had made off and disappeared miraculously through a crack in the wainscot, a crack seemingly far too small for any mouse.

Andy remembered this particular mouse incident – though it was one of many similar skirmishes – because his dad had been furious at their defeat, and at Andy's refusal to obey orders; but then he had reined himself in and not given way to his temper. All he said after chucking the poker contemptuously in the grate (a ridiculous weapon against mice, in any event), as though it had failed him in his hour of greatest need – all he said was: 'They're vermin, son – can't afford to be sentimental about killin' 'em. You'll get used to it, probably.'

Then, all about mice forgotten in a minute: 'Blimey, is it already that time? Don't you wanna listen to "Life with the Lyons" with your mum? It's on now.'

Much later in his life Andy's dad had played a great supporting role when Andy got involved in local football. Every Sunday, fair weather and foul, his dad would be on the touchline supporting his son's team (playing on Hackney Marshes, very likely), though more often than not it was the losing side. He turned up even for training sessions, always ready with encouragement and advice.

The death of his parents was the last memory associated with the family home in Shernhall Street, and they died within ten years (his father) and fifteen years (his mother) of his departure from home to begin married life in Chingford.

Andy's Dad had smoked cigarettes all his life from the age of fourteen; he once confessed this to Andy hoping to deter him from taking up the habit. 'Son, don't be a fool like me. I'm not an old man yet by any means, but I can't run anymore – and I even get breathless walking. You don't want to end up like that, do you? Of course you don't.'

In the nineteen fifties and certainly by the sixties, with the deaths of well-known actors from lung cancer – Bogart was one of them – the notion that smoking was good for you, or at least harmless, was starting to be recognised for the dangerous lie that it always had been. Andy could remember seeing film on Pathe News of Humphrey Bogart being pushed, supine on a trolley, along a hospital corridor, completely out of it.

By early middle age (then a decade earlier than we reckon it today), Andy's Dad had begun to suffer heart and circulatory problems; over the last ten years of his life, things got progressively worse. He began to suffer badly from angina; there were some mild heart attacks and then a severe one. The *coup de grace* was eventually delivered by an aneurism in the aorta.

The day his father died – vivid and eternal in the memory – Andy had been at home with his wife. While he was eating breakfast before starting out with his cab, he was interrupted by a telephone call. Though Andy and his wife had had a telephone for a few years there were still few enough calls in those days that its ringing would be sure always to startle them. This time, Andy dropped his fork and cussed: 'Bloody hell, who wants to be calling this early?'

Jane lifted the receiver and almost immediately turned to Andy and said: 'It's your mum. Sounds as if something's wrong.' Andy took the receiver and heard that his dad had collapsed and that an ambulance was expected soon; the call had been made from a neighbour's house. 'I'll be there soon as I can, Mum,' was all Andy had said.

When Andy got to the house his brother, Roger, who lived closer by, was already there; his face, when he opened the door to Andy, conveyed that whatever had happened to his dad it was very bad. The ambulance had also already arrived. Mum and her two sons were soon together in the "best" room, at the front, where Dad was on the floor leaning back against an armchair gasping for breath, like a drowning man, his skin now as creamy and bloodless as a butcher shop's carcass. The three family members could do nothing but watch in anguish while the ambulance men went about their work. In a matter of minutes Mr Patton was wrapped up and secured in a wheelchair and on his way out of his house for the last time.

But Andy had had time to see that his dad was unaware of the outside world now; his eyes had the look that you sometimes see in the eyes of Madame Tussaud's waxworks; they gave the impression that the man was there, perhaps, somewhere deep inside, but that he was focussed now on one idea or goal or vision which had nothing to do with the outside world, and which you knew must remain a secret for ever.

After about three quarters of an hour in a waiting room at the hospital, a doctor entered and told Mrs Patton and her sons that he was sorry to have to tell them that Mr Patton had died from an aortic aneurism; the vessel had burst causing catastrophic loss of blood. A few minutes later, a nurse or administrative person came in and said something along the lines that it might help if they – Mrs Patton and her sons, that is – decide whether they prefer burial or cremation, and she made some remark about the death certificate; Andy could not recall exactly.

Otherwise a man can't be allowed to die, Andy thought, as his rage mounted. His brother said to the administrative official, as caustically as he could manage: 'We were told only a few minutes ago that he had died, for Christ's sake – we've no idea what we're going to do.' Mrs Patton burst into tears.

Did the hospital really behave so callously or had he misremembered? Andy wondered, doubting the accuracy of his recollection of the details of that day increasingly as the years passed, despite its general vividness.

The family were allowed, or invited, to view the body and took up the offer. People often behave out of character in situations which they have not before experienced – they are caught off guard perhaps; it takes these challenging situations to surprise their inner character into revealing itself.

While Andy and his mum were looking at the body of Mr Patton, the face of which now appeared relaxed and content, all pain and struggle past, and the two of them seemingly at a loss how you were supposed to look at the dead body of a loved one, Roger, who was acknowledged in the family and by his friends – even by his wife – as not a demonstrative, emotional, touchy-feely person, kissed his father on the forehead. He did it as unselfconsciously as an Italian.

Whenever he looked back on this death, and that of his mother's years later, Andy was struck afresh by how unique and out of the natural order of things these deaths had seemed at the time. But death is the most natural of all events in nature, he had to remind himself, smiling unhappily. He had been particularly struck once by the closing commentary in a television programme about the cosmos: that the last event in nature would be a death – that of the universe. Since his middle years these recurring thoughts had usually concluded with a sigh, and Andy saying to himself something like, 'Yes, and it's coming my way soon – but KBO, as Churchill used to say; meantime, let's hope my next customer wants to go to Heathrow and is a generous tipper.'

And Andy had for many years – having thought about it so often – understood and accepted that when *his* turn came, Jane and the children would have a day similar to that when *his* dad had died. Similar not merely in the obvious way of experiencing the unique event of a parent's death, but similar in the unexpected feelings and thoughts that came with the experience – unwelcome and shameful, some of them, when acknowledged.

Andy had been shocked by the news of his dad's collapse but, immediately after agreeing to go to his parents' house, he had thought of how his plans for the day were buggered up and – he had to acknowledge this to himself – there was a trace of resentment because it happened that day and not when more convenient. And he was irritated all over again, but quite pointlessly now, that his dad had been a lifelong smoker.

However, on the plus side, his dad having been a lifelong smoker put him in the wrong, made him guilty of his own demise, and Andy wanted to feel justified in the feeling he in fact guiltily had anyway, that his dad had got what was coming to him.

He was not as upset as he should have been: Dad had been very ill and death was an end to pain and suffering, best for him and for his wife, etcetera. And when he thought about his emotions that unforgettable day, even when he thought about them the very next day, he saw to his shame that he was already fitting his dad into a slot in his own history. Dad had become a figure of the past, Andy's past, even before his son had had the decency to grieve for him.

It was not until much later – long after the funeral – that Andy became aware, and was relieved to discover, he was truly sad that his dad was dead. And in his seventies he now missed him and his mum just as much as he ever had since their deaths. All their little mannerisms, tics, locutions, prejudices – their general unwillingness to accept change and agree that their old ways might, just might, sometimes be wrong or not the best way: none of this impinged at a distance of time – he felt about his parents now much as he had when he was a ten-year-old.

The possibility of a rose-tinted spectacles effect was not something that Andy acknowledged or even considered.

Extrapolating from his own experience the septuagenarian Andy knew, or felt he knew, that his wife and children and friends, when he died, would have the same or a similar experience of loss. First, they would be a little too accepting of his passing despite the dislocation of change, then there would be relief that loose ends were being tied up; but eventually, *soon perhaps, sadness and regret would set it – even over the loss of an ugly, overweight, old nonentity like me,* he thought.

The vanishing forever of anything we once loved and enjoyed, whether a parent, friend or lover, schooldays, the vigour that enabled us to play a sport, an old doll – since they were once an integral part of our life their loss can be experienced almost as a bodily trauma, a deadening of one of our senses, or the negating of our purpose in the world. Andy felt all this, though he would never be able to put into words to his own satisfaction, but was sure too that "things turn out for the best", somehow.

I wonder what Jim would think if I could talk to him about it, or George? Andy would speculate whenever these thoughts passed somewhat imprecisely through his mind.

Once when his girls (three of them, the same as Ben) were in their early teens, Andy had taken them to a safe part of the Lea River to try out a small dinghy they had bought. They all expected it to be fun, and it was but not in the expected way. Andy held the dinghy close to the riverbank while his girls got in and then when he attempted to board – the dinghy really being too small to cope with them all – the inadequate craft listed and tipped Andy, already at that stage of his life beginning to be stout and lethargic, into the drink. The girls managed to avoid even getting seriously wet. It was shallow by the bank, but Andy's spectacles came off in the moment of panic and helpless splashing in the water and were lost. Recovering control of his floundering body Andy was soon crawling up the slippery bank, saturated and muddy, to the sound of ecstatic laughter and hysterical screams from his girls. The river trip was over, but it could not have been more fun. The journey home in the car, with Andy wet and dirty sitting on newspapers, was as happy a time as they had ever had or were to have, together.

They will always remember that day, Andy would often say to himself, always with renewed pleasure at the recollection of the river adventure. It will be for them what Dad and me chasing the mice has been for me. And Mum always letting me eat some of the cake mix before putting it in the tin for baking. And Grandad teaching me to drink tea from the saucer.

What Andy had experienced he felt that his nearest and dearest would too; it does not follow; no reason why it should. But Andy's was a sentimental nature; he believed, rather felt, that everything would turn out for the best; he could not help being like that.

In those clear-sighted moments that we sometimes have, or think we have, Andy saw that when his own time came Jane, his children and his friends would, eventually, come to see him more objectively, warts and all, as the saying goes: *just as I see my parents now in a way I couldn't when young,* he thought. And what they would see they would feel more warmly about – because that was how he had come to feel about his parents. (It did not occur to Andy, because of his nature, that he might not be describing greater objectivity and its consequences, but its opposite: the rose-tinted spectacles vision). However, Andy's vision, for what it was worth, at least was useful in that it caused him no angst, rather the contrary. Because he now saw his own parents, warts and all he thought, and it did not diminish his love for them, instead their foibles and weaknesses, discovered or acknowledged piecemeal down the years, endeared them to him all the more – because of all this his retrospective vision was a comfort. Rank sentimentality, but that was his nature.

Andy once talked to Jim about the strange things we remember from our past – perhaps spoke to Jim more than once on the subject, now he came to think about it – and Jim had argued it more cleverly than ever he could. That was a superiority of Jim's that Andy was always willing to acknowledge. Jim had said something about how our lives' experiences and events sift – that was the word he used – "sift" to essential memories, trivial in themselves perhaps but obviously having special, perhaps hidden, significance for *us*. For Andy, the sifting had left in the panning tray, among many other things of course, the indelible memory of the mouse chase with Dad – more accurately *by* Dad – and the dinghy incident, neither of which had occupied more than a few minutes of his life.

There was an evening when Jim and Andy were in the Bell, off Cannon Street, and Jim had argued a view of the past and how time affected the way we thought about things which Andy did not agree with and still could not accept – but he could not say why it was wrong either.

Jim had made the case (and he would quite likely argue the opposite on another occasion, Andy was only too well aware) that given sufficient passage of time even the record of extreme suffering loses its power to move us to outrage, a sense of horror, or even to sympathy. 'The holocaust still inspires outrage and horror,' Jim pedantically explained, partly, he had said, because it was unprecedented, but also because it occurred within living memory. 'Do we,' he had asked Andy – assuming it would be a clincher of an argument – 'feel anything beyond a general sense of despair over the human record when reading of the deaths caused by Genghis Khan eight hundred years ago? – Said to have been many millions by some historians, and all at a time when the world's population was probably less than half a billion?'

'How do you know that?' Andy asked.

'Google, old friend. The point is – in the long run – for sure in the very long run: nothing really matters.'

To which Andy had shrugged his shoulders and said: 'Well, it's a good point you make anyway, I suppose, even if I don't quite believe the millions figure for Genghis – I should cocoa, as you would say… Does Maureen have to put up with these monologues at home, poor woman? Shall I get another one in, Jim?'

Chapter 8

At El Vino's, after successfully preventing Andy from telling whatever story he had had in mind, the aged drinkers, there being no other topic at hand but unwilling to submit to a taxi-driver tale they were sure they would have heard a dozen times, had lapsed into their default mode: reminiscence about the Minster. If a story was told about the early days at the Minster, it did not matter that it had been heard a dozen or so times before, spread over four of five decades, though only Andy could wallow joyfully in nostalgia about his early days of taxi driving.

The Minster's deputy managing director, Stanley Rogers, to do him full credit, had a middle name that redeemed the quotidian outer names: Fellows; he was Stanley Fellows Rogers. But he was Stan to his friends and to the Minster's managing director, Jimmy Wilson – the latter known always as "the Gov'nor". Though Mr Rogers was nicknamed "Hoss" by the lads because his great size reminded them of a character in the popular Western series of the time called Bonanza. In this horse opera one of the four sons of the family featured was a huge man called, rather nicknamed, Hoss.

Hoss, or Mr Rogers, to be polite, suffered from severe deafness. No one knew why but it was assumed to have been caused by a wartime injury, assumed mainly because Mr Rogers was a respected figure and a wartime injury was something deserving of respect, and his age made it a possibility. Nonetheless, and respect allowed for but put to one side for the moment, Mr Rogers' deafness was the cause of many of the stories recounted about him down the years.

'I remember finding that everybody of my age was earning at least a couple of hundred pounds a year more than me,' George was saying, 'which was a huge amount in those days...'

'A fortune,' Winston interrupted. 'You could've bought about eight suits at Weaver to Wearer for two hundred quid in those days.'

'Crap suits though – we used to call it Weaver to Pauper, if you remember,' Jim said.

Of course, they all did remember because this particular story had come up and been rehearsed, even with the Weaver to Pauper embellishment, at not the last booze-up, agreed, but certainly the one before that – within the past four months then. But what did that matter – it was a good story, and it was their story.

On finding that he was grossly underpaid, George had summoned the courage to ask for an interview with Mr Rogers. This granted, through his immediate superior's mediation – and settled, naturally, to take place after normal work hours – a trembling George was sat one evening a few days later in front of Mr Rogers' desk at the appointed time face to face with his tormentor.

Mr Rogers occupied a small office on the ground floor. The barred-for-safety windows of his office looked bleakly onto the small car park at the rear of Minster House on which the sun never shone owing to the height of surrounding buildings. These windows were invariably closed so as to maintain an ambient tobacco-smoke saturation level suitable to Mr Rogers' needs. Before either Mr Rogers or George had spoken a word during their meeting, George had a coughing fit that brought tears to his eyes.

'Are you all right, lad?' Mr Rogers enquired. 'Would you like one of my Senior Service? He asked, proffering an open pack of twenty.

George knew the protocol, so he politely declined by means of head shaking and a negative handwave while he finished his cough.

What an evil old bastard he was, one of the old geezers would be likely to say at this point in the recounting of the tale, and, in fact, one of them did on this occasion in El Vino's – Ben.

When George had composed himself, Mr Rogers, deliberately looking avuncular across the desk and tapping a fresh cigarette on its surface prior to lighting up, had said, 'Are you happy, lad? Have you got a problem I can help with?'

'So I said to him,' George now said, 'sir, I think I am earning about two hundred pounds a year less than the others of my age... And Hoss said, "Sorry, what's that, lad – what did you say?"'

'So I repeated the whole bloody thing, almost peeing myself by now,' George recounted, 'and then there was a silence that went on for ever. I didn't know what was going to happen. Eventually the old bastard leans forward and says, "Wait a moment, lad, I'll put my hearing aid in."'

'It was a wonderfully effective tactic to put me at a hopeless disadvantage,' George said. 'I ended up saying to Hoss I felt ill – something like that – and could we leave the meeting for the future. And he said, "Of course, lad, don't worry – my door is always open." That was that; I knew I'd never have the courage to do it again.'

'Hoss definitely used his deafness to gain advantage,' Winston said, 'even I remember that, though I left the place still a "youngster" myself.'

The anecdote over, Jim looked at the last bottle of wine, estimated how it would divide into five, and then poured. The cheese and biscuits had been reduced to crumbs by now, crumbs which had taken air and spread themselves across the table so that the unfamous five made you think of elderly rooks feasting at a huge bird table.

'You know,' said Andy, 'I had a similar experience with Hoss...'

'When you tried to get a mortgage – yes? Ben said.

'Yes...'

'I did get one from him,' said Jim, 'so I won't hear a word against the old bastard. I'd never have got on the property ladder if that hadn't come off, I think.'

Winston asked how much he had borrowed.

'Three thousand two hundred. Sounds ridiculous nowadays, doesn't it? But I remember telling my dad, and he was shocked and said, "It'll be a millstone round your neck, Jamie."'

They all laughed – they were always ready to laugh at the silliness of their parents' generation.

'Anyway, KBO as Churchill used to say,' said Andy huffily; 'I'll have another go at trying to tell my story. If you'll give me a chance.'

'Pray silence for Andy Patton,' Jim intoned.

Ignoring Jim's leaden irony Andy took his opportunity:

'Well, I got an interview, like George, and it was exactly the same. I'd explained what I wanted twice before he took the wind out of my sails by telling me to hang on while he put his deaf aid in. Actually, I still carried on. I told him a third time, and he smiled, looked kindly, offered me a fag, and then said he'd look into it. He'd gone through all the usual questions about was I married or getting married, how much deposit did I have, had I found a property, etc. I came out quite chuffed. But I never heard a thing from him – perhaps deliberately or it could just be he lost whatever note he'd taken and forgot all about it. That episode was one of the things that decided me on taxi driving.'

George had remembered something else pertinent:

'It's coming back to me now – one of the things that put me off my stroke when I was in his office hoping for a salary increase, besides him not hearing me of course, was him absurdly mishearing me. It was farcical at times. He asked me, for instance, whether I was thinking of getting married, so I told him I was already married. Then he said something like, "Good. But be sure you've chosen the right girl though: it's too late finding out after you've tied the knot, lad. Don't rush into anything. Long engagements are always a good idea. But you look too sensible to act rashly."'

Their friendly waitress passed by and saw the state of the table.

'Gawd! Looks as if I need to call in the emergency services to deal with your table. It's worse than after my grandchildren's birthday parties.'

The men all laughed, pleased to be interacting with a friendly stranger, and George laughed so heartily that in the act of throwing his hands up in mock horror over the state of the table he then knocked over the remains of his wine – half a glass – to add to the mess. It was worthy of Harpo Marx himself. His friends' laughter increased.

'I can see you're all as bad as each other,' the waitress said. 'As for him,' pointing at George, a soppy-stern expression on her face: 'you ought to be able to control your emotions at your age, my lad – no accidental spillages here, please.' And she winked at George and took away as much rubble as she could immediately, announcing that she would return to finish up soonest.

Jim said, 'We'd better decide if we're having more here or moving on. She'll ask when she comes back.'

None of them could make a decision, so Winston fell back on memories of Stanley Rogers:

'I remember sitting at my desk in the so-called underwriting room – it was only a few yards from the always open door of his office – "My door is always open" – and I could see him on the telephone. More to the point I could often hear him because he'd be talking so loudly. There was one day when I think he wanted to be heard, actually, so that we'd know what a huge salary he was earning. He might have been looking for a mortgage himself when I heard him almost shouting down the receiver, "Salary in excess of six thousand a year – yes, excess of six thousand." It was pure vanity; he knew we were all earning less than a thousand a year. Much less.'

'It was a bigger difference than it sounds nowadays,' Ben said. 'The pay gap – "differential" they'd call it today; Christ knows why, hey Jim? – the pay gap between top management and the plebs was much narrower then than it is now though. Another instance of how things have got worse, I reckon.'

'You sound like me, so I agree,' Jim grinned.

But Winston hadn't finished his recollections of Mr Rogers on the telephone:

'On another occasion, I remember hearing him bellowing at the blower: "In the lower abdomen." About three or four times he shouted it, but I couldn't hear anything else. Had some sort of pain, I suppose, or war wound playing up.'

'Great days,' Jim said, and they all laughed, including Jim, at the absurdity of Rogers' overheard telephone calls somehow representing great days. But they knew what Jim was getting at.

They all, suddenly, were aware of being tired and not able to take this sort of thing as well as they once could.

'Apropos of nothing, George,' Winston said after the group had observed a minute's silence, 'I saw that film *Blood Of The Vampire* on TV last week, the one with Donald Wolfit as the mad medical professor kept alive by transfusions of the fresh blood of the poor devils incarcerated in the asylum he runs. Wasn't that one of your favourites – you and Tony? When I watched it the other night, I remembered you and Tony laughing about it after one of your visits to The Essoldo. Laughing fit to bust. And laughing about it ever after too, more or less ever after it seems to me.'

'Those were the days,' George said, 'yes, it was one of those horror films so badly made that Tony and I did laugh fit to bust, as you say. We got more enjoyment out of it than from much better made films, and more laughs than from most comedies. I still laugh when I think of the two of us in the Essoldo watching Wolfit preparing a victim for the next transfusion and us two streaming tears of laughter. Wolfit was such a good actor – he played it in earnest, as if he was doing Lear rather than tosh; not like Vincent Price sending it up all the while.'

There was another minute's quiet.

They were giving way again to intoxication because of tiredness – they had been out a few hours – and to tiredness because of the intoxication. They had had a fair amount to drink, though it had been spread out over the hours, which had also included some food. At this stage Andy became sleepy and uncommunicative. If he got any worse and began to smile at nothing, as was likely, and then had even more to drink, he could very soon look as if he was doing an impression of an underweight lobotomised Buddha. For his part, Ben would likely become increasingly boisterous, an object of interest to surrounding tables. In Jim, Winston and George, the effects of alcohol and tiredness showed themselves in a desire to provoke disagreement – for the sake of healthy argument not to the point of fisticuffs.

It was no doubt this healthy desire for an exchange of opinions in the unending search for truth, that drove Jim to assert – with apparently no prompting other than the reminiscence about *Blood Of The Vampire*:

'There hasn't been a decent film made since they started doing 'em in colour. All the great films are black and whites. Colour just caused 'em to take their eye off the ball; all they ever thought about after that was: does it look pretty? – Film content went to hell. *Death in Venice* for instance.'

Winston's albino head beamed. The whiteness of his hair and the shining red blotches covering his face made you think of hospitals.

He said: 'Do you want the five minute argument or the quarter of an hour up-and-downer? You know you're talking crap, don't you? Anyway, you've never been much interested in the cinema, we all know that. The "movies", as we who *are* interested call the art.'

'Rubbish, old friend,' Jim laughed.

Winston carried on: 'The next thing you'll be telling us is the writing was on the wall when talkies came in.'

Jim made as if to protest.

'Yes, you will. What you don't get, because for you nothing has been any good since the forties or fifties, or whenever, is...'

'It's got nothing to do with being stuck in the past...' Jim replied before himself being interrupted by George in loud voice.

'Like hell it hasn't. Tutankhamun might be more stuck in the past but not many others.'

And George dissolved in laughter at his analogy. Nobody else, only George. The others smiled, particularly Andy – but then he was smiling all the time now.

'Bloody hell,' shouted Ben, 'who gives a brass monkey? I know what films I like, and it's got nothin' t'do with black and white or colour. They can be sky blue pink with a finny addy border, for all I care. I'm an *Ice Cold in Alex* man meself – the British pulling through in the end despite the odds. Great stuff.'

'Absolutely,' shouted an oldish gent from a nearby table – one in company with a couple of younger, middle aged chaps, all three of whom had obviously had a good lunch, a lunch that brought to the surface their innate tolerance for humankind's flaws, as a good lunch will, unless it does the opposite. Ben had been so loud that half of El Vino's could have given their opinion too, if they had chosen. 'What about *I Was Monty's Double*,' the oldish man added, to raucous support from his table.

Someone from another table, treating it all as a contest now, yelled, '*The Third Man* – that was black and white. What about *the Third Man*?'

A chap who spoke in a way that suggested he wanted to leave no one in any doubt he was gay, said, mock petulantly: 'I can't believe no one's mentioned *Brief Encounter* yet – surely the best black and white of all.

Andy sat silent, emanating contentment, and smiling blissfully but at nobody and nothing in particular, Fleet Street's Buddha for the day.

Winston had another point to make, one he sensed would touch a sensitive spot:

'Anyway Jim, surely at least one of your favourite films was in glorious colour – *Spartacus.*'

'I should cocoa,' Jim answered, 'Slept through most of it, *as you know* – in all probability *because* it was in colour.'

Andy hiccoughed and resumed smiling. Tiredness was having an increasingly deleterious effect on the others also.

George said, 'Before you can comment on a film – using your criterion of colour or no colour, whatever – you've to be able to 'member which it was. I can't always. Was *African Queen* in colour or not? What 'bout *Red River* – hic?'

Their waitress was hovering within conversational distance, sensing that they might need replenishment of liquids and perhaps even of solids, and she suddenly remembered that their table needed a clean-up.

'Is there anything I can get you boys?' she asked, at the same time deftly collecting glasses and plates and wiping away crumbs and spillage, as if challenging them to do their worst all over again.

It would be unmanly, they all instinctively felt, to refuse. More wine and French bread was ordered – the French bread in the belief that it would soak up some of the wine and thereby help them stay sober. Or slow the process of drunkenness.

'D'you 'member the Beamish couple?' George said, out of the blue as frequently happens after wine.

'I 'member it all,' Jim said, nostalgia rising and causing a tightness in his chest.

'Who could fo'get Miz Beamish and Isiah?' said Winston. And, blearily blinking, he added, trying his best to inject satire into it: 'Though we shhud never, never fo'get, Miz Beamish had been a Drayton!'

Jim and George roared with laughter at the shared memory.

'Who...the bejesus are Isiah and Miz Bimish?' yelled Ben, too aggressively. Then, immediately, 'Hold on, I gotta go aunty's urgent. Tell us when I get back...can't wait to 'ear wot I bin missin' fer most of me life.' He tended to revert to the pronunciation and argot of his youth when under the influence or excessively fatigued.

Ben raced off at a stagger. The others looked at each other wondering what might be in store.

'Here we are boys – wine and bread,' their waitress said, pointlessly half filling one glass in front of Jim for him to taste and decide whether it was corked or just great – as if he would have any idea at this stage. El Vino could have got away with red wine vinegar. But Jim went through with the ritual and instantly pronounced the wine, 'Eggslent. Eggslent, my dear.'

Winston was amused at Jim's mental decline, though aware that he too was a bit shaky. He wanted to say something amusing himself, but all that came into his head, though he said it anyway, was: 'Wine and bread: all we need is pries' an' we could do Mass.'

'I need aunty's too,' said Andy, to no one in particular, and headed off.

'Two down, three t'go,' George said.

Jim said, haltingly: 'Jane'll give – give Andy rough time – if 'e goes home – state's in now. He's gone into his walking dead, zombie whatchamacallit mode.'

'I don't s'pose we're in great shape ourselves,' Winston said, swaying gently.

Worryingly – at least for Jim and Winston – George started to laugh hysterically, in full Harpo Marx mode.

'Wasn't that bloody funny, George, whatever you're laughing at,' Winston said. 'Christ, are you gonna have the vapours or something, mate? Pull yourself together or we'll get our marching orders.'

'I've gotta go to aunty's,' George announced, still giggling, and he was off. All he needed was a harp and a stage.

Jim and Winston looked at each other in surprise.

'THREE down,' Jim shouted at Winston, as if he had just got the answer to a difficult bit of mental arithmetic over which they were competing to be first.

By now Winston looked like a waxwork that had been exposed for too long near a radiator on max. Responding to Jim he suggested that they should have brought books with them, to fill in the time while the others were pissing.

'I wonder,' Jim said, 'if these events are 'ginning to get too mudch…too mudch for us…cope with.

Andy was the first to make it back from aunty's. Jim and Winston had started chewing on the French bread, no doubt believing that it would forestall intoxication.

'George still 'ysterical when you saw him?' Winston asked Andy, sleepily, spitting bread crumbs.

'Now you mention it, he was smiling, smilin' all over the place – which is risky in aunty's, isn it? – If I'm allowed t'say that these days. What was it all 'bout?'

Winston could not answer because he had dropped off for the time being, eyes closed, head forward, the muscles of his crumb-laden lips slack and devitalised as though in preparation for major dentistry.

'Shhhh,' Jim said, 'don't wake him. When the others come back let 'em find all three of us sleepin'. Shut y'eyes when I say, ol' friend.' Jim giggled at the prospect of fun to come, almost as uncontrollably as George had been before making for aunty's.

George and Ben soon emerged together from aunty's, Ben looking wan and weary, George looking happy but in a peculiar, static way, his face somehow suggestive that he was now wearing the Harpo Marx expression permanently, as if its glow of loony happiness had been stamped on it by a manufacturer of dolls and nothing now could be done to change the mood.

'Eyes shut, Andy,' Jim stage whispered.

Andy complied and when George and Ben saw the three of them senilely asleep apparently, for a few seconds they were taken in. The ruse worked long enough for George to laugh and say, 'Let's leave 'em here and sit over there, tee hee,' and Ben to say, 'Christ – old gits outing.'

Their waitress was in the vicinity and when she saw the three sleepers – three sleepers at a very far remove from any three graces ever painted – she gave a what-am-I-going-to-do-with-you-boys look at George and Ben and bustled over.

The "two" fake sleepers (Winston *was* asleep) had not been able to keep up the deception for more than a few seconds. The waitress, when she saw what was really happening, before moving off, said:

'Pretending you're asleep at your age is taking a chance, I'd say. One of these days you'll find yourself in the back of an ambulance before you can convince anyone you're okay.' She gave her peel-of-bells laugh and was off.

'She's dead right,' Ben said. 'You've no idea what you looked like. If you *had* been dead, you wouldn't, couldn't have looked worse – silly arses.'

Winston had woken, coincidentally, at the same time as Jim and Andy had opened their eyes. It took him a moment to grasp what had been going on, and he had every intention of pretending that he also had been pretending to be asleep before Jim and Andy spoiled it for him.

Andy said, 'We at least were pretending; it was him –' (pointing at Winston mockingly) – 'fast asleep on his own account, who gave us the idea.'

'Just resting my eyes,' Winston said, winking not blinking.

Jim put up an idea for consideration: 'P'raps we've been sitting here too long. What say we stredch the legs and leg it to the Nell – finish off there?'

It turned out to be a good idea, except for implementation of the first part: getting out of El Vino's. After quite a while spent in getting the bill and deciding to pay it by means of one of the five using his credit card – it devolved upon Winston to do this – and for him to recover cash from the others for their shares, and then more time spent arguing about whether to incorporate the tip by a suitable percentage addition to the credit card payment, which in the end and after heated discussion was decided in the negative and instead they left a generous cash donation separately on the saucer. After all this kerfuffle, there was an eruption of chair scrapping, stumbling, arm waving as jackets and coats were donned, table and chair legs being kicked, and, of course, the toppling of the odd wine glass.

In the street outside El Vino's the old geezers, visibly finding it difficult now to marshal their weakening physical and mental powers, looked woebegone in the November drizzle and cold. They thought of the daunting walk ahead from Fleet Street along the Strand to the Nell Gwynne. They were five refugees on a flight to freedom whose train had stopped between stations and ejected them into the vastness of the steppe. It did not occur to them to take a taxi or a bus; the problem-solving mechanics of their brains had been isolated and muffled in the mental equivalent of cotton wool.

'Keep buggering on,' Andy said, nodding in the direction of the Strand and shakily setting off that way. The others followed – someone was showing a lead, so why not follow it? They found themselves walking into a headwind.

With Andy hobbling on his bunions a few yards ahead, Jim, limping, said to the others, doing his Churchill voice, resonant, lisping, and drunk – the last bit the most convincing:

'You ask me what his policy is? I tell you it is to reach the Nell Gwynne – whatever the cost. And in getting there he offers us nothing but blood, tears, toil and sweat.'

Only Jim laughed. The others had heard it all before, and perhaps they thought it too near the ugly truth: there would be toil and sweat at the least, and with stumbles and falls quite likely you could not even rule out blood or tears.

The drizzle was cold and penetrating; the ground wet and dirty. A tacit understanding broke out to keep conversation to a minimum from now on and concentrate on the goal. The goal, satirised by Jim, was to reach the Nell Gwynne as an unbroken unit. Reach it without anyone falling over and dropping out, or dying of hypothermia on the way; or anyone singly, or perhaps all of the party, being picked up in the Strand by an officious Samaritan-type organisation that spotted the lurching, swaying, stumbling, and falling crew, and judged either one or the whole lot incapable of self-preservation.

The old geezers' daunting and at their age and in such weather possibly perilous challenge, was underway. And they, grim of demeanour, all hoping against hope that they really did have hearts of oak, or the next best thing, that would see them through, were nonetheless dimly, hazily aware that they were stupidly risking their health; it was not worth it even to get to the Nell. Not in their state, at their age, in this weather.

Chapter 9

About the time they were passing the Royal Courts of Justice and soon to skirt round St Clement Danes – occasionally shuddering, slipping, and cursing, and resolutely having ignored all thoughts of stopping for a quick one at the George so near at hand on their left – at this moment in their adventure their better halves were comfortably ensconced in an Indian fusion restaurant in the King's Cross environs. The ladies (four of them only because George's wife had died a few years ago) were at the stage of perusing the dessert menu, never the most appetising aspect of Indian cuisine, fusion or not.

The girls, that is how they liked to think of themselves and describe one another, had met an hour and a half later than their husbands, at half past one. It was not long after that when Ben's wife, Brigitte, the liveliest and most mercurial of the group, and the point of the lunch as we shall discover, had set the tone with her joke, the first of the day. It was delivered in her distinctive enunciation, a mixture of French accent and East End, and perhaps a slight speech impediment played a part too. And the joke was about "fusion" food:

'What eef we 'ad bin to a Transylvanian fusion restaurant – there used to be a Transylvanian or Mongolian one in Covent Garden, I sink: den eet would be a *transfusion* restaurant.' She laughed as if she had never before heard the joke, and perhaps she had not – it only deserved one outing at most to judge from the other girls' immediate reaction.

Her friends soon laughed, though, because Brigitte had laughed so infectiously and because they were all glad to be having lunch together. Nonetheless, Jim's wife, Maureen, said, still laughing despite herself:

'Oh, Brigitte, don't start off with the bar so low. We can *end up* with jokes like that, if we must, but we ought to aim higher than the men at the start. "Transfusion" – that's the sort of joke my Jim might come up with – *would* come up with.'

The wives of the old geezers were meeting – and that they were meeting at all was unusual; they had not met as a group since the funeral of George's wife – because Brigitte had confessed her marital worries to Jane on the telephone, and she had had a brilliant idea. They should meet for lunch, Jane said, all the girls, 'on the same day the boys have their booze-up – that way they don't need to know anything unless we choose to tell them.' *Brigitte's so-called marital worries came as a surprise to Jane – the two of them always looked happy,* she thought; but then, talking it over with Maureen when arranging the lunch, she acknowledged that you never could know what couples were like when not on public display.

Brigitte was not the least put out that the other girls would know she and Ben were having problems. She had picked up on rumours about the others' marriages from time to time over the years.

The girls had known each other for decades, and even if they did not meet with the metronomic regularity of their husbands, still they had met often enough to have maintained a lively interest in each other's lives, and, at a remove, had kept up with events through they husbands' meetings.

Between their own rare get-togethers they derived some benefit, as indicated, of a gossip-knowledge kind from de-briefing husbands after their more frequent meetings. The men, for their part, when they met did not speak willingly or often, and certainly never at length, about their wives – they did not feel any urge to do so and their mates had scant curiosity to satisfy in this department. A whole lunch could pass and no more than the odd question, and that only for courtesy's sake, usually during a lull in significant conversation, would have been asked about "the wife". Cursorily, in passing as it were, it being clear that not much by way of answer was needed. Is Jane still trying to get to grips with golf? Is Brigitte still teaching French at night school? Has Angela's knee recovered after that ski accident? Has Maureen got you to agree yet to cruises as an alternative to flying? A simple yes or no would usually suffice if such a question did crop up.

But a little information, drip fed under duress, and pieced together intelligently and with a dash of imagination (every woman can be a George Smiley when she tries) went a long way with the men's sufficiently intelligent and imaginative wives.

The husbands were often flabbergasted at the extent of what her-indoors seemed to know:

'How on earth could you know that?'

'Well, if she's taken the decision to...as you say she has...then it's more than likely the two of them are... It follows doesn't it?'

'Er, if you put it like that, then I suppose it does – you're probably right. I hadn't thought of it like that – it hadn't struck me.'

'It never does, does it...?'

'Did you get any Old Peculiar at the supermarket, by the way?'

The Ben and Brigitte relationship issue came up quite soon in the restaurant, in fact while the group were still sitting in the bar area, each having a white wine pending a table becoming available. The first matter to be decided, however, after Brigitte's Transfusion joke had been dealt with, was how they would settle the afternoon's costs. Being females they experienced none of the embarrassment that their menfolk would have done, for instance, if one of the old geezers had forgotten himself and started the afternoon by suggesting that they plan how the session's costs should be divided up. Once the cost sharing was amicably decided by the girls – the kitty system was selected; Maureen treasurer – Angela told Brigitte how well she was looking, and how much her new hairdo suited her, and how sorry she was that Ben and she were "going through a rough patch".

'We 'ave bin through a rough patch, yes,' said Brigitte. 'Poor Ben, 'e has 'ad the prostrate, or prostate ting.'

Maureen said: 'God, that must have been awful, but he's in the clear now, isn't he?'

'Through the worst anyway, I should think,' added Angela.

'Yes,' Jane said. 'He is, isn't he?'

Brigitte nodded assent, though not with great conviction.

They clinked glasses on the second pouring of their wine, which finished the bottle and gave them each a modest top-up.

'The trouble is,' Brigitte began, halting for a moment to think how best to put it, uncrossing and then re-crossing her legs the other way, as if indicating thereby that she was about to get down to brass tacks '…the trouble is 'e feels bad a lot of the time – no energy, 'e gets upset at 'aving to go to the loo so often. It 'as made him short-tempered. Sometimes 'e talks, my God, of wishing to be dead. Nothing I says seems right.'

Here Brigitte almost began to shed tears over the situation she had recounted.

The moment passed, however, because a waiter arrived to escort the party to a round table which was near a window but also lit by a small lantern directly above. They were handed menus and left to their own devices, relieved that there was no irritating chitchat from the waiter – that, no doubt, owing to the restaurant being pretty full and the staff stretched to cope. Otherwise, as the girls well knew, they would almost certainly have been asked intrusively whether they were celebrating a birthday, etc., etc., and then felt unable to break with convention and tell the waiter to mind his own bloody business why they were there. Maureen was the only one who might have given him short shrift.

Jane decided that the we're-all-really-in-the-same-boat argument might be a good opener with Brigitte:

'Well, Brigitte, I suppose we all have these bad patches in our marriages – I know Andy and I have. And they can seem like the end of the word at the time.'

'Too bloody true,' Maureen said with feeling. 'I don't mind admitting there are nights when I've gone to bed believing I genuinely hated Jim, and would be glad if he snuffed it…'

'God, Maureen,' interrupted Jane, somewhat taken aback by Maureen's frankness, more that than the opinion itself if she were to admit the truth.

'Well I did, or I have,' insisted Maureen, 'but then, after a day or two, of course I came back to accepting that he was no worse than most. A miserable old basket, yes, but miserable like most men of his age – because he was old because he couldn't do all the things he used to do and enjoy, and there's nothing in compensation for the loss. Yes, Angela, I see what you're smiling at – miserable because that's behind him too, probably, though he'd never say. And…'

'Nothing in compensation?' Angela asked with arch expression. 'What about the joy of grandchildren and all that stuff? Aren't we, the men as well as us, supposed to live on, and for, just that: the grandkiddies?' She said it all with her mock Edith Evans "A handbag?" expression and an irony of tone so marked that it was perfectly clear she didn't believe for one moment they should or could live just for the grandkiddies.

Maureen, whose honest frankness could be deduced from her appearance – hair as grey as nature intended, an outfit which would have done for the model of a WI uniform and some of which was bought at an Isobel Hospice, flat heels, vestigial makeup – Maureen believed none of the stuff about "living for the grandchildren". Certainly, she did not believe – it was her experience – that you could live *only* for grandchildren. If she was honest, and she was, so she did, she would have said that on the whole she did not believe anybody ever lived entirely for the sake of someone else. 'The one exception is after giving birth, I suppose, and that only for a while.' Then occurred to her what she obviously thought – judging from the growing smile on her face – was a mischievous addendum that might shock or at least amuse the girls:

'The Romans, when a birth was going badly and they had to take a decision on who to save…' She dropped her menu on the floor in her enthusiasm for history and retrieved it before carrying on. 'Christ, bending double like that is a real test of the blood pressure pills, I can vouch for that. Anyway, we're told they, the Romans that is, invariably sacrificed the mother and saved the baby, if they had to choose… But we're not told, are we – did they ever ask the mother for *her* opinion before taking the decision?'

The girls looked at each other briefly to check reaction; they found that they were not shocked but rather amused by old Maureen going for it. Brigitte, perhaps because she was a continental, took the question seriously, after laughing only because the others had:

'You will say it is because I am French dat I say zis – too intellectual and all that – but even if the Roman women 'ad agreed, that would only have proved zey were willing to die for others, not dat zey would live only for dem.'

Maureen said: 'It sounds as if you're on my side, Brigitte.' But sensing that it was necessary to bring things down to earth again, Maureen went on: 'If all we grandparents are so besotted with the grandchildren and see no other point in life – have got nothing else in our lives – why are we all bloody-well cruising round the world half the year?'

They all laughed and looked up for the waiter, any waiter, they were ready to eat. Despite continuous chat and laughter each had multi-tasked to the extent of reading the menu.

Jane said her prepared piece: 'My Andy has a saying – he's always saying it. Keep buggering on – KBO. One of Churchill's sayings, if you can call it that. But it applies to marriage a lot of the time; it's what you find yourself doing, I think.'

Angela sighed and said that it was a saying that young people did not take to heart. 'That's why we've the divorce rate that we do. Their motto still seems to be KBO – yes, but all it means to them is, Keep Buggering Off.'

'It's sad, isn't it?'

'Oh, dear, where will it all end?'

'It's not our world anymore, is it?'

Ordering their food was the fraught, confidence-destroying event that it usually is in any Indian restaurant, let alone an Indyfusion restaurant, which listed an Oriental fish and chips, among other unexpected items. They all wanted to order something that they had not eaten before. But none were confident how it would turn out if they made a guesswork choice. They had all risked that at least once in the past and either ended up with far too much to eat or hardly anything at all of substance, or stuff so hot they had to give up after a mouthful. In large company, however, there is always the option of asking for a selection, in this case one sufficient for four people, which was what they all agreed on.

After one or two glances round the large and airy restaurant each of the girls decided, without having to think about it, not to look round again but to concentrate attention on their friends for the rest of the day. Everyone else at surrounding tables, as far as the eye could see, seemed, no, they could not deny, *was* so very young – by comparison. Of course, there *were* men and women in their fifties and sixties, but indisputably that *was* still young – by comparison.

It was not merely the age issue that hit home when the girls had looked wanly about them. There was the obvious truth, which it took but one look at the other tables to take in with a clarity and certainty which left no possibility for self-indulgent misinterpretation. The others in the restaurant – all of them it appeared – were still active players in the game of life. It was not over for them. It had not yet degenerated, as for the girls it had, into a mere matter of shopping, scanning holiday brochures, arranging wills, passing wealth down the line to avoid death taxes, discovering what dose of statins best suited, finding out what on earth it is that the University of the Third Age does, going out for social lunches, and – of course – looking after grandchildren.

Food arrived and for the time being it took their minds off how far they were down Cemetery Lane, which ought to say something about how fitful, tenuous, trite perhaps, exaggerated, is our relationship with death. If a stack of onion rings – that was the girls' best guess as to what those things were in the middle of the table surrounded by dips – can blot all trace of what you were thinking about, even if what you were thinking about was death, then how significant can it – death – really be? Not very. For most of us death is only a serious consideration when it is happening, like, say, appendicitis, which we do not think about until it happens. Death emerges into peripheral vision as we reach old age. Of course, you might have a professional interest; thoughts of appendicitis will cross the mind of a medic often enough. And priests seem to think of little else than death; for them, too, it is a matter of professional obligation.

Of the four girls, Maureen was the most at ease socially in a group. She had been a secondary school teacher until retiring at sixty; for her, a one to one was still something she had consciously to work at, whereas in any group larger than three she fell naturally into the role of chairperson, moderator, or principal speaker – usually all three. The other thing she was not good at was handling people who disagreed with her, despite the practice she must have had at home sparring with Jim. Again, this was most likely because schoolteachers do not have to cope very much with children who tell them they are wrong. Thus, schoolteachers inevitably develop a false sense of omniscience, or at least have a strong tendency to.

The girls having made up moderate-sized plates of food from the selections available, enough to make do for a main course, and Maureen, irritated, having waved away the waiter who had asked prematurely whether everything was satisfactory – 'We've no idea yet as we haven't had a chance to eat anything!' – then Angela, the topic of grandchildren still in her mind, and still smarting somewhat because she and Winston did spend a lot of time cruising, opened her challenge: 'Coming back to what you said Maureen, I think you could say that oldies cruise for half the year – those who can afford it – so as to be in peak condition to cope with the nippers for the other half. Minding grandchildren and nothing else in your life...no cruising, nothing much else...well, it ends in the funny farm most likely.'

'Let's not get side-tracked,' Jane said, seeing Maureen looking as if she had been hit below the belt, her lesson rejected. 'We're here to give Brigitte the benefit of our marriage counselling. Something like that.'

Marriage counselling was evidently a module within Maureen's syllabus; she pulled herself together and addressed class:

'I think the key to keeping men happy in marriage,' she said, her hands now clasped in front of her on the table, her plate pushed to the side for the lecture, and eye contact being made with all the girls in turn systematically, 'is to remember that they are just like us; they need to be spoken to and to feel we're really listening to them, interested. Now, the problem is, all our girly mags have got it the wrong way around. They're constantly giving us articles featuring moaning minnies who tell us that the spark has gone from their "relationship" because their *husbands* – or partners more like – don't communicate with *them* anymore. The good old empathy's gone – blah, blah, blah.'

Angela interrupted: 'No, Maureen – you can't have been reading the articles recently: like any time in the past ten years, I'd say. Nowadays, Maureen, the articles are all about the mechanics of sex – the process not any psychology: how to fit this bit to that bit, and when, and for how long – what buttons to press, and at what stage in the business. Talking! Well, that doesn't come into it, unless you count dirty talking and how and when to do that.'

Everyone was now interested, very interested – there might be a real up-and-downer. And about a proper topic, a topic for all time, not Brexit, North Korea, Trump or some other here today gone tomorrow tosh.

Brigitte (who *should* have been the most engaged after all) despite the accuracy of Angela's criticism of Maureen's knowledge of girly mags, thought the latter had made an important point about communication.

'It's true, as Maurine says,' – Brigitte couldn't help pronouncing the name this way – 'my Ben often complains dat we never talk like we used to…'

An inspired Jane had to break in: 'Remember when we were young and in love and hung on every word our lover uttered, and…'

'No!' said Maureen, but evidently joking, and the others laughed; and Angela added, still laughing herself, that it was all too long ago to remember 'if we ever did talk much.'

'Very funny, but you know I'm right,' Jane said. 'Look at any young couple who've got the hots for each other…'

'Ugh – what a horrible expression,' said Maureen sourly, banging the palms of her hands on the table to show her disgust.

'…Look at any young couple whose hearts have been pierced by cupid's dart. Is that better, Maureen?'

Maureen said, 'Much.' And she looked genuinely placated.

Jane continued:

'One of the ways we recognise that two people are in love is that they're obsessed with each other. When one of them talks then the other drinks in every word, desperate to miss no subtle inflexion, and the eyes of both are locked on their target, the lover's eyes. Talk, yes, talking, it's an indispensable part of the falling-in-love process. And, agreeing with Maureen, the talking bit seems to be as important for men as for women. When you probe friends who boast that their partner is their soul mate, I've always found that how they explain it is revealing. They do so by using expressions like "He seems to know what I'm thinking", "We decide everything together", "I can always tell him what I'm really feeling", "We like the same things", "He's always interested in what I'm doing", "We always discuss things"… What they never say is, "He's my soul mate – fantastic in bed".'

'It could be they're being diplomatic,' Angela said.

'You don't believe that yourself, Angela,' Jane said.

Maureen thought it was time to summarise the lesson, lest anyone should have missed the salient points, but principally Brigitte.

She did so, and when satisfied that Brigitte had had time to take it all in, she directly addressed her:

'The thing then, Brigitte, is this: have you and Ben lost the habit of talking, genuinely talking to each other – and also listening to each other?'

'Is difficult to explain…'

'God knows it's easy enough for it to happen,' Maureen carried on, just as if Brigitte had not answered, or attempted to answer. 'Over the years at any rate. I find it difficult beyond measure sometimes to listen to Jim moaning about the same things… What the bloody hell's inside this batter I'm crunching through, I wonder?'

'Chicken,' she was informed by Angela.

There was always something reminiscent of Winston in Angela's demeanour and dress. Partly, it was that she dressed expensively and drew attention to her clothing by frequently patting or adjusting it. She also had Winston's capacity to disconcert, seemingly unintentionally: the effect of her words often bore little relation to their face value. On this occasion her "Chicken" had sounded more like a threat than a clarification; but you could not have said with any certainty that she had intended it that way; it was her peculiar effect. Winston might have picked up this manner from his wife, of course, not vice versa, except that his oldest friends could vouch that he had been the Winston they knew ever since they met him, which was long before his second marriage.

Maureen continued, unintimidated by the unintentional threat:

'Anyway, there's a new vape shop in the town replacing our only fishmonger, and I just switch off completely when Jim starts on about it again. And he isn't listening half the time when I'm speaking. A good deal of the problem is that we know each other so well that we hardly have to say out loud what we think: I know his opinion of vape shops, and he knows what I think about modern methods of teaching history. And if something new comes up, I only have to look at his face to know what he thinks. In the euphoria of first love, this telepathy is all very well – novel and enjoyable; we feel empowered, as they say nowadays. Later, though, it's a curse.'

'So 'ow do you deal with it?' Brigitte asked eagerly, prematurely feeling grateful to her friend because she believed that an answer was on the brink, about to be vouchsafed.

Maureen said:

'Well, we can't sit around mum because we know our significant other is only too familiar with what we think about almost everything under the sun.'

Maureen's serious and pedagogic tone disappeared instantly as she realised, with great surprise, that she had no answer, despite having been a schoolteacher. She presented her damp squib of a peroration with hockey mistress brio and jollity:

'I suppose what happens is that we must each carry on talking (it's a difficult habit to break – ha ha!) – accepting that our other half usually isn't listening. And that's marriage, folks. Da Daa.'

Like a music-hall comedian using a well-tested technique for winding up and exiting the stage, Maureen roared with hollow laughter – all she lacked was a straw boater. She was, however, embarrassed and ashamed at finding herself – having chosen her own route after all – up a dialectical cul-de-sac.

Brigitte looked perplexed, imagining she had missed the point.

Angela said:

'Perhaps the answers come in lesson two.'

Jane said: 'Brigitte, don't get confused. The talking cure *is* the answer; but talking is the means not the end. The end is making, in this case Ben, feel important. Like a lot of men in retirement…'

Maureen immediately interrupted:

'Jane, you've hit the nail on the head…'

Angela groaned and pleaded:

'For Christ's sake, give someone else a chance, Maureen. Carry on Jane.'

'Excuse me for breathing,' Maureen said, and she ostentatiously leaned back in her chair indicating she was out of the proceedings until further notice.

'Like a lot of men in retirement,' Jane continued, 'Ben probably feels he has no place in the world anymore. From being someone deferred to by his staff, who was looked to for decisions that would affect numerous other people, and who had all kinds of other responsibilities, he suddenly found himself a nuisance who was always under your feet around the house. And who runs the house? Who takes all the decisions? We do: the wives. Leaving aside domestic abuse for the moment, there is no equality in the home: women rule the roost. So what is Ben, or any husband for that matter, to do in retirement to retain self-respect, a meaning to his existence – especially if he doesn't play golf?'

Maureen decided she was back in the proceedings:

'It sounds as if you're going to say that hubby has to be allowed a big say in when and how to clean the house, the design of the new kitchen, what cleaning materials need to be shopped for; that he should be left to maintain, say, the Christmas card list, the record of the children's and grandchildren's birthdays – indeed, keep a look out for items of clothing that the grandchildren might need and buy them as presents… Oh no. That way lies chaos. If your husband's name is Jim, it does. He can't work the dishwasher or the washing machine. Can't bleed the radiators. He used to change washers on taps, but not in the era of the ceramic-type whatchamacallits. And now that you never find a ball cock in a lavatory cistern, they're a closed book too.'

She once again banged the palms of her hands on the table to signal conclusion, but she stopped short of announcing Q.E.D. She'd learned her lesson – *a* lesson.

The selection of Indian and indeterminate items, probably from other cuisines, was by now devastated; so, eventually, they came to wondering had they had enough to eat? No, they decided, though they all agreed that about half as much again would do. Maureen tried to signal to their waiter, but in vain. Only after numerous and increasingly wild attempts to catch his eye, all of them cleverly evaded, so he could get on with tidying piles of menus, sorting cutlery, whatever, did he condescend to notice; and then he feigned urgent intent to meet their needs. He strode rapidly to their table. The girls' order was simple:

Maureen said, 'We'd like the same again but half portions – is that possible?'

'Of course, of course.' Then the waiter foolishly added: 'Is it a birthday party today or some other little celebration?'

Maureen paled but quickly recovered.

'Not quite,' she said.

An insane glint had come into her eyes but she nevertheless spoke to the waiter earnestly, no trace of twisted humour observable.

'I've been diagnosed with a cancer of the womb and given a week to live. This is a farewell lunch.'

Then she looked into the distance abstractedly, ethereally – as ethereally, that is, as any woman in rude health could.

'Oh – I'm... Would you like another...?'

'Yes, just one bottle before I go – sorry, before *we* go.'

'Well done, Maureen,' Angela said when the waiter was out of earshot. It was just her kind of humour.

'Yes.'

'Yez.'

They all laughed.

In the distance, their waiter looked on admiringly. *What courage these old ladies have,* he thought; *they broke the mould when they made that generation.*

Jane was first to compose herself and look serious again, an odd and sobering thought had occurred to her:

'We've spent most of our lunch talking about men, our husbands, and why they're not happy. But do you imagine that during their lunch today – largely liquid – there'll have been any talk about us, the plight of women and the role of wives? Apart from the odd "Cor – look at her" when a fit young one passes by, there won't have been a look in for the gentle sex.'

Angela pointed out that they were here trying to give Brigitte the benefit of their combined understanding of men's failings in order to help her sort things out with Ben, 'Who as far as I comprehend Maureen and Jane, following our deliberations, just needs to be treated like a human being, and then all will be well twixt the said Brigitte and Ben.'

'No, no, no, that's not fair at all.' Maureen said.

'That's an insult to Brigitte,' Jane said.

Brigitte said: 'I do treat 'im like a 'uman being – you 'ave got it wrong there Angela.'

'Sorry, but there ain't no point shooting the messenger: I'm only summarising what was said.'

'We said nothing of the sort,' Maureen averred. 'We…'

'For a start, Maureen, you told us that Jim couldn't be allowed any responsibility at all in your domestic affairs, which, correct me if I'm mistaken, is the status a slave would have – if we still had slavery…'

'*Reductio ad absurdum*,' interrupted Maureen, confident that Latin would win the day.

'Rubbish, Maureen – with due respect…what I glean from what you've said is that it's no wonder marriages breakdown if one party is reduced to near slavery. Of course, before telling us that Jim can't be trusted with anything now he's retired you did agree with Jane that making Ben feel more important was the key to solving her domestic situation. So where do we go from there? I don't see how a slave can be made to feel more important – that's my point. Jane eloquently explained how redundant men, retired men, feel in the home, and Maureen, you seemed to be making the case that they should be kept that way, despite earlier saying that Ben must be made to feel more important. Well, listening to the two of you I couldn't get anywhere; so I fall back on my principle that in getting on with anyone it's a matter of respecting them as human beings. Not the sort of answer that would get mileage in *Cosmopolitan*. But that's what it always boils down to – in high politics and in the home. Unfortunately, in the home, familiarity breeds contempt – and there's much more familiarity in retirement than when at least one of you is out earning the daily bread.'

'What are you telling me, den, Angela?' Brigitte asked reasonably.

'We're all too old to solve marital problems by taking another trip down the old primrose path of dalliance, so why not start – and I'd give Ben the same advice if he were here – by making an effort to be more polite and friendly, by talking to him in the polite, interested way you talk to your neighbour over the fence, and by not taking his opinions and behaviour for granted as if it were your right. It may be your right, but that's beside the point. I ain't got nuffink else ter say, me gel. Probably shouldn't have said as much.'

Jane said: 'Brigitte, it'll all work out in the end. Being ill and old takes getting used to, and that's Ben's situation.'

'Jaw, jaw – not war, war; there I agree with Angela,' said Maureen.

'Talking – if nothing else – passes the time,' Angela said; 'it's what we're doing here, after all. We like meeting and talking to each other… Second best is listening to Maureen lecturing us!'

They all laughed, including Maureen, and enjoyed feeling on good terms with one another.

'Let's have pudding,' Brigitte said, 'if dey has anysing good. I hope so; it's my favourite.'

This time the waiter was at the ready, alert to the needs of the old ladies as if Maureen and her dear friends were the only customers in the restaurant. This is a farewell meal, he was keenly aware. 'What a brave gutsy trooper that old lady is!' he said to himself, running to their table.

Chapter 10

The five old men, intrepid in their way perhaps, but anything but the picture of intrepidity – not a lantern jaw among them, nor a fearless piercing gaze, nor an upright, rigid back or swift striding gait. They were passing King's College, the five of them, as a close-knit group – no straggling or charging ahead by individuals. Perhaps they were coalescing, as penguins do, for warmth and protection against the wind – though it is unlikely that they went the whole hog (whole penguin) and rotated the centre spot of the huddle to share warmth, as penguins do.

When this Nell Gwynne expedition reached the archway entrance to Somerset House, also the location of the Courtauld Institute, Andy suggested that they take shelter under the arch, just for a bit, now that the rain had become heavier. No one demurred, so they shuffled into an untidy group outside the Courtauld shop and stood there looking suspicious but at least protected from the rain and wind. Winston was the only one to bother looking through the window of the shop.

'Why do art gallery shops always make such a big thing of flogging women's scarfs? What's the special connection between scarfs and art?'

Ben said: 'Who bleedin' cares, for Christ's sake. I just want to be inside somewhere warm that's got the basic facilities of civilised society – like an aunty's.'

'We could all do with one soon, I suspect,' Jim said, anxious to quell any sign of disagreement that might lead to the group splitting up or to Ben going awol. 'We'd probably have to pay an entrance fee to use the Courtauld's aunty's. The only one I can think of, and the Nell itself isn't much further off, is the Strand Palace Hotel – especially good if you need a crap. I've never risked that in the Nell – it'd be like crappng in a submarine,

I imagine. The Strand Palace is good because it never makes you feel you're being watched.'

'A mine of information,' Andy said.

'He should be editing Time Out or something,' was Ben's surly response.

George said: 'Let's bite the bullet and get to the Nell in one go.'

'Listen,' Winston said, excited, as one who has all of a sudden made an important discovery, 'we've all got our bus passes on us, haven't we? Why didn't we think of it before we got saturated? We're only yards from a bus stop and buses that go down the Strand.'

'Cos we're all pissed,' Ben said, bleary eyed but with renewed motivation. 'Come on then, let's get a bus.'

With that, Ben was the first off the mark. He had a burst of energy as well as, or perhaps because of his pressing call of nature, and he ran off heedless whether others followed. Within seconds, as his friends could see, all of them now having reached the opening of the arch at their own more stately pace – within seconds, Ben had flung himself into a number 26 bus that was about to depart. Ben's friends watched, mystified by the turn of events but interested how it would turn out. Jim muttered, but to himself rather than his friends: 'It's a number 26.'

The bus turned left after a couple of hundred yards. Unsurprisingly as it was on its usual route across Waterloo Bridge. Ben would soon be much further away from the Nell Gwynne than he had been since leaving El Vino's.

Andy was the first to laugh but the others rapidly joined in. Jim had to take off his spectacles to dry his eyes; Winston lifted his left leg and slapped his thigh in joy; George had to lean for support against the wall. Passers-by smiled to see the old fellows really enjoying themselves despite the inclement weather. Perhaps old age had its compensations.

It took a full two minutes for the men to recover their usual composure, and it was only towards the end of this happy interlude that the thought of what might become of Ben and the rest of their afternoon broke upon any of them.

Before these thoughts were to occur to Jim, he had remembered a lunch a few years' back when they all had discussed how differently men and women react to surprises such as they had just now experienced. Upsetting, frustrating or amusing, depending on your point of view.

But that was the point. Would you be more likely to think it upsetting because you were a woman or amusing because you were a man, or vice versa? They concluded (it did not worry them that a woman's opinion was not involved) that, yes indeed, gender did play an important role. There had been a bit of a shouting match, Jim remembered – nothing unusual about that – but he could not recall who had most strongly advocated the gender distinction – either me, Winston or George, he assumed.

Anyway, so he remembered, there had been some psychobabble, from one or other of us, which had carried the majority with it. The theory had been advanced that men had a stronger sense of the ridiculous because they were more likely to recognise that there was no particular point to existence – that whatever happened did not in the end matter. Whereas women, because of their biology – creators and nurturers of new life, and all that – could not afford to view life as pointless or ridiculous, or ridiculous because pointless. Hence, if a group of old ladies had witnessed one of their party inadvertently catching a bus that took her in a totally wrong direction, they would, assuredly, not have collapsed into a paroxysm of laughter. They would have shown concern for the plight of their friend.

Jim still thought that on the whole women would be upset by such an incident, not moved to hilarity; but reflecting on their old discussion he realised that he and his friends had offered only the flimsiest explanation of why. Embarrassing. *Still,* he thought, *whether you laugh or cry over it – it makes no difference to Ben at the moment: he's where he is now – t'other side of Waterloo Bridge; and it's up to him to find his own way back.*

'He's going to end up by the National Theatre before he can get off, and if he's got any sense he'll have a pee there,' Winston said.

Andy said:

'God help the bus driver: he'll probably get abused, or beaten up, for going the wrong way.'

Andy was still finding it all amusing and had another good laugh imagining Ben's furious response at finding himself on the wrong bus.

George persuaded the others just to set off for the Nell and let Ben sort himself out. They needed little persuading.

'He knows where we're going. He's grown up. He'll find his way back – eventually. Someone send him a text and tell him we're in the Nell keeping a urinal free for him.'

'I'll text him,' Jim said, 'but let's get going. I'll do it on the hoof.'

Whilst he was limping and texting, the reduced party of four crossed the dangerous approach road to Waterloo Bridge, landed on the main stretch of the Strand, passed Simpson's on their left, saw the Strand Palace Hotel on the other, north side of the road, and decided to give it a miss and hold on until they reached the Nell. The Nell was only a couple of hundred yards further on, just past the Vaudeville Theatre.

Jim's fat and arthritic fingers had managed, but only with difficulty and many corrections, to compose a text to Ben, whose mobile, he knew, was always turned off unless he expected a call. Jim was satisfied that the wording would succeed in its twin aim of showing concern and causing irritation. It read:

'We'll be in the Nell if you'd care to join us later in the day. Act in haste, repent at leisure!'

On reflection, Jim thought it didn't cut the mustard on the 'concern' front, but he had sent it anyway. 'Bugger all likelihood anyway of him reading it before tomorrow,' he said, addressing the wind and rain.

Ben liked to be upstairs when on a double-decker bus, but the view up and down the Thames from the top of the number 26 afforded no pleasure today. There was no time. As soon as he realised that he was being taken across Waterloo Bridge, Ben leaped to his feet and raced downstairs to be ready to get off at the next stop, wherever that might be. And he could not remember where it might be, for the life of him, in his present agitated state of mind. Why does it always happen to me? He was confused. He was so confused, indeed, that pictures of the Elephant and Castle, the Imperial War Museum, and the Old Vic, floated before him as possible disembarkation points. The movement of the bus, especially when he was thrown about when trying to get down stairs, had made him feel queasy – he had drunk more than he should. *It's not fun as it used to be,* he thought: *just stressful and exhausting. I need an aunty's.*

There was relief for Ben when the bus came to a stop and the doors opened. He was off before anyone else and thankful to find himself only a little way over the river, and the National Theatre looming in front of him. He decided to visit the NT aunty's before finding a way back to the Nell. Better safe than sorry.

As he was making his way down the stone steps to river level his mobile, which for once he had forgotten to turn off, pinged. *Bloody hell,* he thought, surprised as usual that anyone should contact him on his mobile; *I suppose the cooker's blown up or the house has disappeared into a sinkhole.* But it was Jim's message. When he read it, Ben was not irritated, nor did he pick up any sense that Jim was "concerned" – but he roared with laughter. Typical Jim, he said to himself – 'care to join us later in the day.' Ben laughed because he knew, and he knew that Jim knew he knew, there were many stories of Jim's own capacity to create hilarious cockups arising out of his absent-mindedness.

On the way through the crowded foyer of the NT heading for aunty's, Ben was thinking of an insurance industry association conference they had both attended years ago. Neither had known that the other was attending until they met by chance at tea break in the afternoon. They were pleased to see each other and would have fallen immediately to chatting had not Ben already been in conversation with another conference attendee. Nonetheless, Ben hailed Jim when he saw him, placating the chap by his side with an 'Excuse me for a sec, an old friend of mine.'

Jim ambled up to Ben and his companion, and Ben said, when Jim was within earshot:

'How's it going so far?'

Jim replied, as expected: 'Rubbish.'

If Jim had been the type to leave it at that, he would not have had the reputation he did for getting himself into embarrassing situations. Jim did not leave it at "Rubbish", he went on:

'I was at one of those tables at lunch where all the other people are less animated than tailor's dummies. You won't believe it, but I've no idea who I was sitting next to and the lunch went on for an hour and a half, though on our table it seemed half a day, I promise.'

Ben was laughing at Jim's tale but the chap next to him looked stern. Ben thought he would break the ice:

'Jim, you obviously haven't met Mike here, who's a director at Winterbourne's; Mike, this is an old friend of mine, Jim Anderton, of the Minster.'

Jim confidently agreed he had never set eyes on Mike. Mike, however, took Jim's proffered hand and shook it, a tad coolly, saying:

'We have met, actually, Jim – I was sitting next to you, on your right Jim, at lunch – today.'

Ben guffawed as he pushed open the door of aunty's – he'd got to the end of his recollection. 'I was sitting next to you, on your right, Jim,' he mumbled while standing and waiting patiently, playing over in his mind once again that scene from the conference, and smiling the while.

Ben's four friends reached the Nell Gwynne before Ben had even entered the National Theatre. They were glad to be somewhere they knew so well; there would be no surprises; they knew the routine and were safe. Though there was one surprise, but that was for the Nell's barmaid cum manager:

'You back again,' she said, wide-eyed, looking at George; 'isn't once a day enough anymore?'

'It's a long story,' George said, 'and if you don't behave yourself I'll bore you to death with it.'

Winston said slowly, loudly and emphatically:

'Never put your lobelias out until May is over.'

'What?' the barmaid said. 'Come again?'

Winston repeated himself:

'Never put your lobelias out until May is over.'

Then he responded to the barmaid's questioning gaze and explained himself:

'You've got this sign on the counter here, requesting, rather starkly if you want my opinion, "Tips". Well, I've just given you one: Never put your lobelias out until May is over.'

The barmaid knew he was harmless, despite his weird blinking – she had seen him and *all* of them often enough.

'What can I get you?' she asked. 'And don't ask for Sanatogen again – or you might find it's what you end up with.'

They ordered their preferred brews and a G and T in anticipation of Ben's arrival and while she was drawing their pints she asked:

'Where's the one with the broken nose?'

Andy answered:

'He had an urgent appointment on the other side of Waterloo Bridge – in a little room at the National Theatre, I assume. It shouldn't run on for too long. We're expecting him here any minute. The G and T's for him.'

The barmaid could not get why the others were tittering at Andy's explanation, accompanied as it was with stagey winks and nods, but it was unimportant. She left them to get on with their beers and returned to washing glasses.

Everything about the Nell satisfied the old men's needs in a pub, except for the two televisions suspended high up in opposite corners, always on, always tuned to Sky news or sports, and always on mute.

'I'm obviously too old to understand,' Jim said, now they were sat around one of the few tables in the pub, the one underneath the portrait of Nell Gwynne herself. The others knew what he was going to say because they could see he was looking at one of the televisions. They had heard it all before.

'Does anyone at home watch television on mute? So why do they do it in pubs? It's irritating, isn't it? – You look at it and don't quite understand what's going on and want to hear. But you can't. You'd be happier if the bloody thing wasn't on.'

After downing the first refreshing quarter or thereabouts of their pints, each man reacted as if he had been slipped a Mickey Finn. Walking to the Nell from El Vino's had sobered them, they felt – but they were mistaken. It had been one step forwards on the road to sobriety, but the first slurp of their next pint in the Nell had sent them at least two steps backwards. It was a sign of their age, they all knew that much. Once you had had enough (and enough was not very much at their age) – then you simply had to stop or you would go downhill fast. Even if you took the odd break – eating, say, or moving to a different drinking hole, the benefit was marginal. Unfortunately, none of them had the moral courage to say: That's it, if I have any more I'll be falling over.

Jim saw that the others were not drinking with enthusiasm. He knew they felt like him. But like his friends he was not about to say anything sensible on the subject. This moment of genuine empathy – of actually sharing the feeling of those around him, *knowing* that it was their feeling as well as his, transmuted into a surge of warmth and affection for his friends.

These three tired old men – they looked it now, in spades – whom he had known as youngsters; whose energies, aspirations, opportunities, abilities, health, he had witnessed slowly eroding down the years, until there was little left of any: he felt for them. He was not so dull either as to be unaware that there was in this whoosh of warmth a dose of self-pity. Everything had eroded for him too.

Andy now saw a dishevelled Ben push his way into the small bar through its only entrance and seek his friends, whom he knew would have "had such a laugh at my bloody expense", and would do so again now he was back with them. They had at least done the decent thing, he spotted, and provided him with a G and T.

Winston asked: 'Tell us, then, Ben, why you needed to go over Waterloo Bridge to find an aunty's?'

'I just needed to get away from you lot for a while. I'd forgotten for the moment that other people are also bastards. Anyway, Cheers!' He downed most of his G and T and did it with more relish than the others in tackling their beers.

'Where did you find an aunty's?' George asked.

'Oh, yes – the bus stopped on the bridge above the National Theatre, so I went in there.'

Ben remembered something that had either interested or surprised him about his visit.

'I saw something interesting while I was there. I looked at their programmes and some of the promotional videos showing on screens, and stuff, and saw that they're doing a Macbeth set in the 1950s in a Butlin's holiday camp. The clever idea, as far as I could make out, is that Macbeth, who's a Butlin's redcoat, and his wife, who's also part of the entertainment team, kill the Butlin's manager, called Duncan of course, so as they can then rule supreme in Skegness. They do this after three drunk waitresses tell Macbeth that he could be boss if he plays his cards right: that's what sets him thinking. But that's only the beginning.

'The trouble starts when the ghost of Duncan, the old manager, suddenly appears, though he appears only to Macbeth, if you know the story. Yes, he appears in the middle of the knobbly knees contest. A spectre that only Macbeth can see, sitting in an empty seat at the judges' table. And no one can understand why Macbeth gets into a tizzy.

'I've never gone for Shakespeare, as you know, but this production sounds like it's got something going for it, a real laugh. I think I'll ask Brigitte if she's interested. Probably find I've put my foot in it again, though.'

Ben was articulate and bright considering how much he had drunk. The excitement of his detour to the NT was what had pulled him round. His friends, however, were beginning to experience what they called "the blur", which needs no explanation for anyone who has once been intoxicated.

Jim said, but only after making a great effort to break out of his new torpid state, 'Macbeth in a Butlin's holiday camp! I should cocoa. Now I've heard it all. As Macbeth himself said, "I have lived long enough. My way of life is fallen into the sere, the yellow leaf…" Bleedin' Jesus.' He dropped out of the conversation for a spell; he was tired or, who knows what? – Old, that was enough reason.

'God, I feel old,' Andy said; 'perhaps it's the time of year and the weather.'

'No,' said George, 'you feel old for…same reason I do – 'cos you are old, mate. You don't imagine you're going to feel younger next spring, do you – just because it is spring, mate, not winter? It'd be nice, wouldn't it? But we've had our good times Andy. That's…truth. We did have good times, though – many people don't.'

'Yes. Did. Great times.'

'We've all had a lot to drink t'day,' George slurred, 'so what I'm sayin' is prob'ly crap, but the old days at the Minster were the best I had. It wasn't school days that were the happiest – far from it in my case – but the old Minster days.'

Winston and Ben were listening but had nothing to contribute for now. Jim may have been listening but he also had nothing to say.

George said. 'When I think back t'when I was a teenager and earlier, and the things I enjoyed then, it's hard to credit now – retro…retrospeculatively I mean. No kid would put up with it nowadays. On a Saturday, or maybe a Sunday, Mum and Dad'd decide – not every weekend mind – that we should have…we should have day out. Either a trip up west, which meant walking up and down Oxford Street window-shopping. The highlight for me was having a tea and cheese roll in Lyons or the other one – the ABC.

'If it wasn't going up west, our day out I'm talkin' about still, then it'd be a trip to a museum or art gallery that was free, free entry – the National Gallery, the British Museum. They were the most likely. It was a sex education, of sorts, for me, as a ten-year old, to look surrep...spishiously at Bronze... Bronzino and Rubens. I didn't get much of a look 'course; my parents rushed passed 'em once they'd spotted at a distance the, to them, "gratuitous" nudity. That was the word Mum always used when she was in her Mary Whitehouse mode and talking about sex on telly, in the cinema, in the newspaper, pretty well anywhere – "gratuous". I'm not sure even now whether in Mum's opinion there was anywhere where sex wasn't gratuous – gratuitous, I mean.

'Are you still awake, Andy? I'm finding it a bit boring meself, mate.'

'Still awake, just about,' Andy replied. 'It was prob'ly still a sex education for you, in those far off days, when they were taking you round and you were fifteen! He.'

George too was now feeling weary. His head felt heavy. He chuckled at Andy's joke, just out of politeness, and leaned back in his chair and stared uncomprehendingly at one of the televisions, already having forgotten what he had been talking about.

The five of them sat without speaking for two or three minutes, only one or two of them sipping drink now and then. A couple of them were staring blankly, following George's example since he became mesmerised by the mute television; the other two gave the appearance of turning something over in their minds, but whatever the problems were that they wrestled with, no third-party input was needed.

None of the old men looked uncomfortable with the long silence. Like contented married couples of long standing these friends had developed over decades a trust and contentment in each other's company that begins in those silences and is ever after reaffirmed by them. They are a proof of close intimacy rather than, as for those who are neither close friends nor lovers, evidence of social awkwardness, wariness, fear. That the old men could now and then nap without embarrassment, a couple at a time or singly, in a pub, that was a shared bond too.

George soon fell asleep – 'Just resting my eyes,' he would have said if woken to buy his round – and he dreamed of being in the London Stone pub in Cannon Street, opposite the railway station of that name. This narrow corner pub, long since destroyed though the name persists, was popular in the sixties with the Minster lads (girls rarely went to pubs at lunchtime in those days), as it was only a short walk from Minster House in Arthur Street and it was a change from The Bell.

In his dream, George was holding a good spot at the Stone's bar counter. The pub was crowded. There were three cheese rolls on a plate in front of him, and he was holding a pint of bitter. In company with him was Les Rogers (it was several years before he was to decamp to Herne Bay) who had bought a similar lunch. The cost of the three cheese rolls, each containing half-inch thick blocks of cheddar, was covered by the daily three-shilling luncheon voucher issued to Minster staff. Les smoked and would sometimes exchange his luncheon vouchers for cigarettes, strictly illegal but many shops were happy to do it in those days.

The two friends were at the pub that day, in George's dream, because there was a test match on and the London Stone was one of the few pubs that had a television – a small black and white job resting on a high shelf in a corner. At lunchtime during tests, the television was always on, and George and Les were keen on cricket.

"Always on" is not quite true. In his dream, George was saying: 'I wonder if we'll see Barrington get his ton before he turns it off.'

'Once this latest bunch has been served, I reckon he'll flip the master switch,' Les answered. 'Barrington's got to get a four off this over or we've had it. We won't see it.'

The "latest bunch" were a group of scaffolders – four of them – from the Cannon Street site. The station was rebuilt in the early sixties.

Les was correct. No sooner had the barman, Duranty (so nick-named by the Minster lads because of his large nose and general resemblance to the American entertainer, Jimmy Duranty) – no sooner had Duranty taken payment from the scaffolders for their pints (the drinking of alcohol not a health and safety issue on building sites in those days) than the manager of the Stone exercised his commercial nous. He always sat leaning with his forearm on the bar, his back against the wall, in a corner where the highly polished wood bar counter met the wall at right angles. In this position he could survey his whole pub without having to move his head more than a few degrees either side. When the pub was full with men holding drinks, but some of the drinks only half pints, and most of the men looking at the television and supping but rarely, the manager would switch off the electricity to the television. He had installed a master switch under the lip of the counter in the corner where he sat. He masked his mean action with an open copy of a newspaper spread in front of him.

This behaviour was sadism in the opinion of George and Les. But its practical effect was to remind customers to drink their drinks, which they always did when the screen went blank. And within minutes the pub would be half empty and ready to welcome new customers who wanted to find out how England were faring in the test, and who would have to buy at least one drink for the privilege.

George and Les knew the routine. They would wait it out. Buy another pint if necessary. The television would usually be on again after a drinks interval of five or ten minutes.

This part of George's dream played in his unconscious like an old well-loved video. If he remembered it when he awoke, he would not be able to say, "How strange dreams are". But George's dream today moved on and now found him sitting in a grubby old café called something like Parascondola. He could not be sure, ever, that he had the name right even when he remembered it awake. (The café was not being an invention of his dream.) It was not peculiar, therefore, that he could not be sure of the name in his dream either.

Parascondola, or whatever it was called, was in Dowgate Hill, off Cannon Street, which runs down the right-hand side of the railway station to Upper Thames Street. In his dream George was sitting in the cafe with his father, about which he felt strange, probably because he had never actually been there with him. It was a highly improbable event as his father had never worked in the City and rarely ventured there. The two of them were sitting at an ill-lit table the surface of which was greasy and littered with crumbs of cake and bread. They had cups of tea before them and some cake. The atmosphere was steamy owing to the lack of ventilation and the constant pouring of boiling water in the making of tea. His father, wearing a bishop's mitre, looked serious and said to him:

'George, son: You never know – you never know… Always keep your powder dry.'

This was advice George had received from his father on many occasions when awake, but never was it imparted so pithily as in the dream. The two precepts had never before been delivered together, stripped of embellishment, superfluous words. Just the core message, lapidary. In his dream George imbibed this fatherly wisdom solemnly as if he was the initiate in a tribal rite of passage.

When awake, however, George used to joke with his friends that the expression – "You never know", appeared to be as far as his father had delved into the meaning of life. And that "Keep your powder dry" was the keystone of his philosophy – either that or, George would say, 'the foundation stone to which bugger all other stones had ever been added.'

'Somebody wake up, for Christ's sake,' Ben said irritably and in a voice much louder even than the conversational volume necessary to compete with the pub cacophony.

'Just resting my eyes,' George and Winston said in unison, rising unenthusiastically to full consciousness. Jim and Andy had been hovering between the conscious and the comatose worlds.

Once roused to full consciousness Jim opined, pompously of course, that as a group they may no longer be that which once moved earth and heaven but – so what! – they were still…still one equal temper of heroic hearts.

Andy looked at him askance.

'P'raps you've woken up a bit too quickly, old timer. You ain't makin' much sense to me ol' china. Talkin' in tongues is what they call it, ain't it?'

'All 'bove your head,' Jim said, laughing. 'Poetry. Tennyson.'

'Patronising old git.'

'It only seems patronising because you're too thick to know what I'm talking about. What I said wasn't intrinsi…in itself wasn't patronising… In the old days it used to be called – what you've got a galloping case of, my friend – an inferiority complex. Nobody ever suffers from it nowadays, though – not since it's become politically incorrect to have it or notice that anyone else's got it.'

Ben advised the two of them to give it a rest – 'Put a sock in it!' – And he did so with such vim and such a glare that it did not cross their minds to dissent.

'We need another pint to pull us round,' Winston said, 'a round to bring us round.'

It could not go on much longer. Something had to give.

George pointed out that they were only half way through their current pint, though Ben had finished his G and T. The others acknowledged a fair point and set to with determination. The slight recovery from intoxication they had earned by their walk from El Vino's was indisputably ceded to a severe relapse when they finished their remaining drinks.

Another round was ordered by Winston, after he had struggled to his feet and become mobile – no one could remember whose turn it was, and he was nearest the counter. The barmaid had no tray to hand and told Winston she would bring the drinks across. Winston seemed to take up a lot of space in the small bar, slowly, ponderously, and unsteadily making his way back. He was happy when he plopped into his chair. So were the other customers.

'We're all going t'have mum and dad of hangover tomorrow,' Winston said.

Everything was in slo-mo now. Any comment had to wait slightly longer than usual for a reply, as if the conversation were taking place via satellite.

'The hangover's a necessary evil,' Jim said with drunken dogmatism. 'If we didn't have hangovers, it'd be because we didn't drink.'

Pause.

'Is evil necess'ry then?'

Jim looked as if he'd been goosed.

'Not this sort of argument again…Christ's sake,' said Andy. 'We've had enough for today. Why don't we ever discuss football transfers, like normal men?'

Pause.

'Not normal,' giggled George.

Long pause.

'I don't feel normal at the moment, that's for sure,' George said. The flesh on his face seemed now to be hanging looser than ever.

Then George decided to tell his friends a bit of his family history.

'Don't know whether I've ever told you – just occurs to me; think you'll find it funny. Whatever. You're goin' to bloody hear it anyway. During the Blitz, my dad was on leave (he was in the navy) and staying at what was my grandad's house then, in Clapton. He'd been out one night with his old friend, a Liverpudlian who'd come down for a holiday to London – during the blitz mind – sounds bonkers, I know – he must've been on leave too, I s'pose. Anyway…'

'This is all leading somewhere,' Winston asked, blinking furiously.

'Anyway, after closing time, Dad and his friend Frank – always Uncle Frank to me – by the way, he took me and my brother, Uncle Frank took us, that is, on holiday to the Isle of Man once – must've been in the early fifties. Anyway, back to the Blitz. Dad and Uncle Frank came home blotto and went to bed in the back bedroom…'

'"Back bedroom" is a key detail, no doubt…significance of which'll be evident – eventually,' Winston interrupted.

Jim gestured to Winston to be patient. George continued:

'Anyway, dad and Uncle Frank went to bed – *in the back bedroom* – in its double bed – no suspicion need 'ttach to that fact in those days – and there was an air raid later that night.' George paused for breath and to take stock of where he was in his story. 'There would have been an air raid warning, 'course, and there was an Anderson shelter in the back garden, but I'm not sure anyone ever used it. Anyway, to get back to the nub, a bomb dropped nearby, but the house escaped direct hit – or so they all thought. Grandad and his wife (second wife as it happens: his first died young of TB) were also in the house. Anyway, point of the story is that come mornin', Grandad went into the back bedroom to wake Dad and Frank and discovered – discovered, that the sash window, frame and all, had been blown in by the bomb and landed on the bed – woodwork intact but the glass…glass, 'course, shattered. The two men were still fast asleep under blankets and window...the shattered glass and window frame. Joke is, it hadn't disturbed their sleep when it landed on them.'

There was a pause while everyone took it in.

Winston broke the silence:

'It could only've happened in the *back* bedroom. Obviously.'

'You tell a story then.'

'Who am I? Bloody Scheherazade?'

'It's a good story,' Jim said, straightaway off into his comic fantasy, 'a story about the generation that fought and won, against the odds. Fought so that Islington might be gentrified and England free to choose Tony Blair and David Cameron as Prime Ministers. Fought so that we might have the X Factor, Ant and Dec, Desert Island Discs, the thoughts of Russell Brand. Fought so that Jeffrey Archer might be elevated to the House of Lords, Andy and Fergie might marry, Iraq be blown to smithereens, and sheep may safely graze in the Falklands. All this and more – much more than this.' His last sentence Jim sang, as near Frank Sinatra as he could: 'We did it our way!'

It was the spur to get Andy singing, ironically of course, in a croaky high tenor:

'There'll always be an England, while there's a country lane.'

The others joined in:

'Wherever there's a cottage small, beside a field of grain.'

Andy had started in too high a key and by the time they got to "field of grain" they were all at the top of their registers. It stopped at that point in a bout of coughing and spluttering. But they had enjoyed it and other customers who had looked to see what was going on did not enquire further when they saw the age of the group singing that song and causing that noise.

The old geezers took a draught of what for them was as good as any blushful Hippocrene: bitter – before you had touched a new pint it even had the beaded bubbles winking at the brim. Sometimes, Jim went so far with Keats as to agree his notion of drinking and leaving the world unseen. Perhaps he and his friends would do so today.

When they all had recovered some remnant of dignity and composure, following their singing and coughing, Jim said –

apropos of nothing: 'Do you think our dads felt like we do, when they were in their seventies?'

'How *do* we feel?' Ben asked, as if he'd been personally insulted by the question.

'Like shit,' said George, 'though I don't know whether...whether I speak for everyone,' he finally got out. He spoke like one delivering lines he was reading or had memorised.

Winston was not so drunk that he failed to see something amiss in George's behaviour – something apart from mere drunkenness.

P'raps we've had enough,' Andy said.

'We'd had enough an hour or two ago,' Ben replied defensively, his alcoholic tendency causing fear that the drinking session might be coming to, for him at least, an untimely end. The weakest link in the chain, Andy, might be breaking. 'Another drink can't make us feel worse than we do and may pick us up.'

Jim said: 'Fine, but it'll be my last today. Yep, last t'day.'

Ben put his hand up for this one and creaked into the upright ready to launch himself at the bar.

Winston chose this break to venture down the steepest of staircases, steeper by far than that at the Slug and Lettuce, to access aunty's.

The narrow staircase at the Nell begins its descent, vertiginous immediately, through an opening in the wall in the cramped space at the side of the bar; in height and width the opening fails to cut the mustard; regulars at the Nell tolerate it as an amusing reminder of the submariner's cramped existence.

The staircase drop, besides its sudden start, adds the extra challenge that it falls left almost instantly once you are on it. The overall tunnel effect is created by the narrow drop, reflecting the width of the opening, being walled on both sides, and a ceiling low enough to make even a man of average height have to duck until he reaches the bottom. Once there, at the foot of the stairs, you have to do a rapid left turn and then another even quicker one, before it becomes at all worthwhile – or safe, indeed, because the ladies loo still has to be got past – to begin searching for the zip on your flies. And that, of course, always needs as much elbow room as you can get.

It was a cramped situation in the basement, indisputably, and Winston, who did not like enclosed places at any time, would soon, as he knew well from past experience, irrationally believe he must be at least ten feet below the level of the Thames and hopelessly vulnerable. And always when in the Nell's aunty's, and taps were on, pipes gurgling, and a cistern filling up, he would be certain he heard the river's waters pounding their banks and slapping against superannuated rotting stanchions. Panic would only just be held in check, if he was lucky.

Chapter 11

Whenever he thought about his irrational behaviour in cramped and enclosed spaces, Winston recalled his father's mental problems in the last decade of his life and wondered whether he would go the same way. Though when his father died age seventy-seven, he was in remission from what he himself, in his coherent periods, always called his loopies.

Dan Cryer's loopies began when he was in his mid-sixties. It came as a terrible shock to Winston and his mother; it must have been terrifying to Dan too. The first Winston heard about it was when he was phoned by his mother: she told him – too scared to think about breaking the news gently – that:

'Dad's funny, son, he keeps telling me to shut up and that "they" are listening to everything we say – through the electrical sockets. There's no reasoning with him. He doesn't let me answer the phone or talk to the neighbours. I'm only phoning now 'cos he's in the loo. Oops! Got to go now – he's coming back. He'll be furious if he finds out.'

Winston had no idea what to do – phone the doctor, the police, or go see for himself. He would have phoned the doctor except that he could not be sure what would happen if he did. Heavies barging into the house unexpectedly was not what he wanted – mainly for his mother's sake. He decided to go and assess the situation for himself.

What he went through after arriving at his parent's house, a thirties semi in Watford, was an entirely new and wholly unpleasant, disturbing experience. As soon as his father answered the door, Winston saw that he was not himself. He did not look like anybody normal. Ever after that day, whenever Winston heard people talking about mental illness as if it were something other than mental illness, he became near mad himself. You hear all kinds of crap, he well knew, like, 'What we call madness is only an unusual rational response to a mad world.' Etcetera. Always he would tell the offending party:

'When you're in the presence of someone in the middle of a mental breakdown ("nervous" breakdown if you insist), you don't have any doubts about their condition: you know they've lost their marbles – temporarily maybe, but that's what it is.'

Winston in due course had the full experience of coping with a loved one who had lost it, as we now say. What he remembered most clearly was that it was all immediately indisputable. When he arrived at his parents' home after that chilling call from his mother, all doubt was dispelled in a trice: his father did indeed believe that the authorities, whoever he thought they were, were listening through the electric sockets. But that was not the only communication issue; the television and radio were not to be turned on because they also gave the authorities a means of listening in and sending subliminal messages.

Once, on a rare occasion when his mother was able to talk to him without his father being present, she told Winston that his dad had locked her in the garage for an hour – she had been found talking to a neighbour and had to be punished. Things eventually deteriorated to such an extent that Winston, with his mother's agreement of course, had to get his father certified – a process that entailed, in those days – perhaps still does – getting two doctors to assess the patient and agree that he was a danger either to himself or others and had to be removed, by force if necessary, to a secure mental care facility.

The night his father was taken against his will to a psychiatric ward (persuasive argument gained no traction with him) was not without incident. Winston's father was convinced that "they" – the conspirators – were getting the upper hand, and he was determined to do what he could to escape. His efforts when being inducted at ward reception included landing a right hook on the chin of one of the male nurses who was endeavouring to prevent him from running amok. Winston witnessed the episode; he had stayed around to ensure that his father was properly treated – not abused, as he had heard sometimes happens with mental patients. The mental nurse was down for a count of about five, had anyone been counting. After a great struggle, during which his father evinced the strength of a strong young man, the team of medics managed to administer a sedative by hypodermic injection.

'Those were the days,' Winston chuckled, somewhat uneasily, not entirely convinced, as he was gingerly climbing the ladder back to the bar. He had no more idea what he meant by the remark – "Those were the days" – than anybody else could have done had they been privy to the thoughts he was reflecting upon. How often, it suddenly occurred to him, do we old people say, "Those were the days" and mean, at most, nothing more than, "That was when I was in my prime", or "I had that particular experience – no one else did", or "It was good then, better than now, despite what was going on?"

It was good to surface from aunty's, though in doing so Winston only narrowly avoided being hurled down the stairs before he had a chance of putting a foot into the bar. Ben, in a great hurry, coincided with him at the Wendy house entrance and had no time for civilities as he barged past.

The next thing Winston was aware of was that the very loud voices he could now hear – appropriate in volume if offering advice to a football referee a hundred yards away – were those of his friends at the other end of the bar. 'Christ!' was all Winston muttered. He stood where he was and listened. Then he heard Jim shouting:

'The royal family are all Germans anyway – they'll be forced to leave the country after Brexit! Ha! Ha! You can't be a democracy if the head of state gets the job by right of birth.'

Andy screamed back at Jim, who was only about four feet away across the table:

'Who's going to be bloody president then, some twit like Alan Titchmarsh or Stephen Fry?'

'Why not? They couldn't do a worse job, and democracy allows you to evict the useless at intervals, my friend. That's the key point: you can get rid of 'em.'

'So it would be Titchmarsh, eventually sacked, followed by Fry, followed by Neil Kinnock – Gawd 'elp us! Big deal. Sooner have the Windsors.'

The excitement of anger, and the surge of adrenalin it caused, saw the drinkers conquer their slurred speech for the while.

'A smattering of history wouldn't do you any harm, Andy – it's not something you necessarily pick up in the back of a cab though.'

'What a pompous, four-eyed git you can be, Jim. Early dementia, I suppose.'

Unflustered, seemingly uninsulted even – Andy was his friend, after all, Jim continued:

'Two world wars blighted the twentieth century and they occurred because the most powerful European countries at the beginning of the twentieth century were monarchies. Not only were they monarchies, they were closely related families – their monarchs all grandchildren of Victoria.' Jim waited a moment for it to sink in, then drew himself up and concluded with oracular confidence in his knowledge and understanding:

'The first world war was caused by the jealousy of the Kaiser for his cousins' possessions and of their status in the world. And if there hadn't been a first world war it's certain, I think, that we wouldn't have had Hitler and the second round.'

Winston who had now begun his tussle through the throng halted again when he heard an outsider contributing his pennyworth of comment on Jim's thesis. Such interventions had happened in each of the three other venues they had visited today, and Winston decided he would hover and see how this new exchange between his friends and the rest of the pub progressed before he returned. What the outsider had said, apropos Jim's explanation of the origins of the first bout with the Hun was: 'Bollocks!'

Winston felt sure that such had been the opening salvo from conversational interlopers in the Slug and Lettuce and the Punch, earlier in the afternoon, though he could not be sure. He did, however, remember that one of the interventions had concluded in an unseemly brawl; and that was followed by a fortunate misunderstanding by the management, and then a hasty embarrassed exit by himself and friends. They had got through, as Kenneth Clark famously said, but only by the skin of their teeth.

'An intervention from the floor,' Jim yelled, his face glossy and red, his eyes crazy, 'pray silence, so that this spokesman for the next generation' (the man was middle-aged) 'may expand on his insight that we talk – he does not mince his words: Bollocks.'

The man looked like a boxer who has been hit several times by punches he did not see coming; but before he could reply, George said:

'You'll have to excuse him. Do you remember that television programme *The Good Old Days*?' The man nodded. 'Well Jim, here, used to be the stand-in compere. So you'll understand why he talks in that irritating music-hall way. He can't break the habit.'

The man, who had splintered off for the time being from the couple of drinkers he was with, had a sense of humour.

'Oh, indubitably, with the certitude of irrefragability I concur your postulates.' He roared with laughter at his own performance. He too was three sheets to the wind. 'But my "bollocks" comment relates to your' – and here he pointed at Jim – 'saying that the three monarchs were grandchildren of Victoria: they weren't. George and the Kaiser were, but the Tsar was a cousin of theirs only by marriage. I lecture in twentieth century European history, so I know. Don't know much about anything else maybe, but I could give the exact blood connections if you were interested. Not a lot of people are, as Michael Caine might say.'

Winston, accompanied by Ben, who had also safely returned from the underworld, interrupted Jim's dressing down. The history lecturer returned to his own group. Winston said, exaggerating absurdly, 'I could hear you, Jim, while I was at the urinal, yelling about the bloody Saxe-Coburg and Gotha and Battenberg cake dynasty, or whatever they were called, before they rebranded as English and took the name of a famous soup.'

'Yes,' Ben agreed, scowling. 'We need to keep it down a bit.'

All five were sat around their table again but the noise in the now crowded bar meant that conversation between them was easier if conducted separately in two groups – Ben and Jim next each other on one side of the table, and Winston, George and Andy squashed in the window corner across the table.

Jim had forgotten about his history lesson and said to Ben:

'Seems like ages ago we were making our getaway from the Punch. How are you feeling now, ol' friend?' He continued without waiting for an answer, perhaps fearing he would not get the positive one he wanted. 'Everything passes. Even troubles at home do. My considered advice, old friend, is stick it out. Brigitte's a good person; you don't want to upset the apple cart at your age. You're going through a bad patch with your health, so you're seeing things, as they say, through a glass darkly.'

'Yeah, but it's not always me that's wrong.'

'Doesn't matter. Bite the bullet. Don't react aggressively. Try it. It might become a habit.'

'What's the point of developing new habits at our age?'

'You've got me there, ol' friend.'

The pub had become noisier than ever. From their table none of the men could any longer see the bar counter or much of the dresser behind it, or even one of the televisions. The crowd was so tightly packed that standing drinkers were leaning against the backs of the chairs occupied by Ben and Jim.

On the other side of the table, Winston said to George:

'On the train coming in today I was thinking for some reason, as you do, about the trip we had to Devon and Cornwall. It suddenly struck me in a way it never has before – I just hadn't thought about it, I suppose. It struck me that we're all now twenty or more years older than the Beamish couple were; that is, than they were when we stayed in wherever it was and thought they were really old, decrepit people. So old that we wondered how we should talk to them, address them – do you remember? – As if they were a different bloody species. Frightening.'

'I wasn't there so I can't speak,' Andy spoke.

George thought about it for a moment, seeming to have no notion who the Beamish people might be. He knew who the Amish were but who were the Beamish? Then it flashed upon him. 'Oh, yes, Isiah with the stroke and Ma Beamish, once a Drayton, with the towels round her legs. Those were the days. You're right, I still think of them as an elderly couple, though at most they were, what? – in their late forties or early fifties, I reckon.'

Winston said: 'I'm surprised you could hardly remember, George. We've talked about the old Beamish B and B once already today, haven't we – with Jim? Or perhaps not: maybe I was just thinking about them.'

'Christ! We've had a few drinks, Winston. I'm not exactly amnesiac.'

Andy interrupted their tiff:

'Look around you,' he said, fiddling with his trainers again, in the end lifting his heels out of them to get some relief. Not that anything could be seen but the backs of fellow drinkers. 'Some of the punters here are in their fifties. I bet if you could read their minds it'd be clear they thought it wasn't worth us getting up in the mornings.'

Andy sat back smiling, slumped, Buddha-like – his feet felt better.

'Couldn't disagree,' Winston laughed. 'I wake up thinking the same. Some days.'

George said: 'We wonder why we should get up in the mornings because there's nothing for us to *do* any more. Now we're retired, I mean – other than please ourselves. And even pleasing yourself palls after a while…'

'But does it – if you really are doing what you please?' Winston probed, hopeful of finding a weakness.

'It does in my case. We're close to – no, past, our sell-by date. P'raps the younger people can tell from our smell, the way the out-of-date human product has dried up, shrunk, crinkled, gives off an odour.'

'Yeah, you are a bit whiffy and off colour, George,' grinned Andy, and they all laughed. In fact, George went so far as to say, 'You've got to laugh, haven't you?'

Because they *were* still laughing, Winston said: 'We bloody are laughing, aren't we?' extending the joke and the laughter.

Across the table, Jim overheard scraps of conversation from other groups nearby, Ben being quiet for the present; and a phrase and a word that always lit Jim's blue touch paper, especially when used in a particular context, cropped up in the scraps he could hear. One was "bucket list" and the other "artist".

Jim had the impulse to interrupt the conversations in which these hated locutions had occurred, but he needed to be sure which group they had come from, and it would be helpful to have an idea of the context in which they had been used. Neither proved discoverable, so Jim cooled off. Nonetheless, all that he might have said ran through his mind. He had thought deeply on the subject over recent years, and even bored his friends from time to time with the fruits of his cogitations.

The film, *The Bucket List*, starring Jack Nicholson and Morgan Freeman – which came out in 2007 – Jim had seen and enjoyed. So had Maureen, who had gone with him. But long since then Jim had formed the opinion that today's "bucket list" obsession – people, nowadays, being more likely to have drawn up a bucket list than a will – was commercially driven.

Yes, he affirmed to himself now, his lips moving in sync with his thoughts, *in former times (pre The Bucket List) an old person when told that death was close at hand and inescapable would thence (nice word, "thence") be advised to look to his or her spiritual welfare, endeavour to come to terms with that old imposter death, go about serenely taking a last leave of friends and loved ones.* Jim's lips stopped moving.

But the old way is inexpensive, Jim eventually had realised. And this recognition had led him to his discovery of the commercial inadequacy of the old way of facing death: it implies an end to conspicuous consumption after you have received the death sentence. Much better for business and the economy, Jim saw, if the market can persuade you to run from the consultant's curse straight to your desk, there to draw up a list – the good old bucket list – of the ten expensive jaunts you intend to cram in before the evil day. Especially now you can calculate your finances to last out your predicted span. Jim's lips began moving again. But he was talking to himself only.

God, all that hanging around at Heathrow…and only a few months left! And then on your death bed: there you lie, one of the unlucky ones, cursing because you got through only eight of the ten must-do's on your list. Now, on your deathbed, in the corridor of an overcrowded hospital, it is clear you shall never see the Grand Canyon or white-water raft the Zambesi… Will St Peter admit you through the pearly gates if your list is incomplete? We are assured that God's mercy is infinite.

Jim was smiling now; he wished he had had the chance to fire off his tirade at some deserving party – or anyone.

'What you grinning at, Jimbo?' Ben asked – he had had a minute or two himself that he could not have accounted for. With his broken nose and his shaven head shining like polished steel now he was perspiring, he looked, even as a septuagenarian, not someone to mess with.

Jim was startled back to mundane reality.

'Me? Nothing really.' And then:

'Did you hear a twit over there, near the fireplace, talking about some footballer as "an artist"?'

'No. But so what?'

Jim was slightly deflated – really too tired for argument.

'It doesn't matter.'

'What doesn't matter?'

'What I was saying. About someone calling a footballer an artist.'

'P'raps he paints as well. Why shouldn't he?'

'Paints as well! Dear God. Priceless!'

'Well, Churchill used to paint. Did bricklaying too.'

'Christ!'

'You started it.'

Jim started laughing but only out of a feeling of helplessness.

'Did bricklaying too!' he repeated.

'Well he did. Why shouldn't a footballer be a painter in his spare time? Like Churchill. Or be a bricklayer, if he wants.'

'No, no,' Jim said, approaching exasperation now. 'I meant – they meant; whoever said it over there – that he was an artist *while* he was playing football. Geddit?'

Ben looked at Jim, missing the point – he'd had a lot to drink; he didn't geddit – and decided he was being made fun of.

'Jim, I don't know where all this is goin' but even I know that no one could paint even Picasso's three-headed women and play football at the same time. What's the joke, 'cos I'm losing patience?'

'Beam me up, Scottie. BEAM ME UP!'

'What's going on over there?' Andy yelled – literally yelled, the noise level was such that only cotton mill communication was sure to work – provided you had mastered lip reading.

All Winston, George and Andy could see was Jim laughing hysterically and Ben not seeming to be in on the joke. Both of them also looked distinctly the worse for wear. Of course, Winston, George and Andy, sitting more or less side by side, could not so easily see themselves. Before Jim and Ben could gather their wits to make a reply, Andy moved awkwardly – he said he felt cramped in the corner, the corner beneath Nell Gwynne's portrait – and knocked a pint glass from the table to the floor. It failed to break and it had no more than a third of its

148

precious liquid remaining before the glass hit the deck. Not a disaster – there was no broken glass – but it was George's pint, not Andy's.

Chapter 12

The four wives took an unconscionable time deciding from their dessert menu the offering with the least calories. They thought they had succeeded several times, but whenever a selection was made they became distracted by a fresh topic of conversation and promptly forgot their preference. Now that the Ben and Brigitte matter was done and dusted everyone, including Brigitte, was more relaxed; there was more laughter, there was frivolity, there was a feeling that they could be a little bit irresponsible now – they had earned it.

Angela was enjoying herself so much, feeling so expansive and at one with the world, that in a moment of private conversation with Maureen she apologised if she had been curt or sarcastic earlier in the afternoon. However, she neatly deflected, or dispersed at least, some of the blame from herself, saying that nobody could live with Winston for thirty or forty years – 'Sometimes it feels like a hundred!' – Without a little of his 'innate acerbity' (that was how she described it) rubbing off on them.

'He's coming over again,' Jane said, meaning their devoted waiter. 'It's make your mind up time.'

Two had lemon sorbets; two had vanilla ice creams; all opted for cappuccinos to accompany them. On account of her impending death the waiter was particularly attentive and charming to Maureen. She wished now she had not begun the fiction but knew it had to be carried on to the bitter end – end of their meal, that is, and departure. Angela made things worse for her by asking if she realised that none of them would be able to use the restaurant again: Maureen because she ought to be dead, or at least have a convincing explanation for her miraculous recovery; the others because they might be asked about the funeral and 'how you coped at the end.'

'They say it never pays to lie,' Maureen laughed.

'I 'ope Ben and the others are on their way 'ome by now,' Brigitte said.

Jane pertly observed: 'If they're not, they'll say they stayed on to avoid the rush hour traffic.'

'Well, we're still here, aren't we?' Maureen said – though we did start an hour later.'

'And we've had a meal in a restaurant,' said Angela. 'If they've remembered to have a sandwich it'll be something to put in the diary.

Maureen laughed but then became pensive.

'I wonder when they're going to act their age? None of them are up to these long sessions in pubs and wine bars, not any longer. On the other hand, it's difficult to visualise them meeting for a formal lunch in a restaurant and sitting around for four or five hours and not getting, well, not getting blotto, as Jim describes it.'

'They could all go to the Tate – Tate Britain of course; hardly the other place – or the National Gallery, and enjoy each other's company while taking in the art.' That was Angela's suggestion, delivered in such a way that only she could have confirmed or denied an element of irony.

'They could all go to a cricket match together, or they could take up bowls.'

'Dey always has interesting talks at zee British Library.'

What these old ladies did not consider was that they, like their menfolk, were doing what they were doing because at their stage and station of life this was what they found themselves doing.

Their husbands did not meet and socialise at the hunt, or "the club", or regimental dinners, or at Henley, or at health spas; nor did they dine out nightly, have a box at the opera, and spend their winters in warmer climes. They were still on the railway lines that they had found themselves on when teenagers, and these took them where they would. Of course, it is always possible to jump train and try to go in another direction, and in every generation a few energetic and lucky souls manage to do this. But for men of the generation and background here under observation, the probability of changing lines was scarcely higher than that Prince Charles would derail and end up in a chicken-plucking factory.

Maureen could have told her friends of all the obstacles to progress, both in work and socially, that young Jim had faced: obstacles often risible in retrospect. She had told them previously, so could not again today, of one of the risible. How when Jim had started work and first been asked to make a telephone call, he had broken out into a sweat. How is it done? He had the number, which consisted of a few letters followed by the numbers. He knew that you put your index finger into the spaces on the circular dial corresponding to the letter or number wanted – he'd seen it done in many films – and then you turned the dial clockwise until it met opposition. He did this and was sure that he'd put in all the correct letters and numbers in the correct order – but then what? Nothing happened. He had forgotten – no, worse than that – he did not *know* that you had to lift the receiver from its place of rest first, *then* dial. Someone – a girl too (Oh, the shame!) had witnessed the whole failed operation, and she laughed, and she explained, loudly, so that others present could not fail to hear, exactly what he had done wrong and how you *should* use a telephone. Jim saved what face he could by cutting short the girl's explanation as soon as he had twigged the mistake: 'Blimey, stupid, I just forgot,' and he shook his head in disbelief at his own absent-mindedness.

There were no telephones, or bathrooms or running hot water, sometimes no indoor lavatories either, in the homes of ordinary people in those first post war decades. Nor did ordinary people ever feel comfortable in hotels or restaurants – they could never be sure that they were behaving properly, not unwittingly guilty of a solecism that betrayed their class. Unless a child was a genius, university, which would have accustomed him or her to the social mores of other classes, was not an option. In this context, "him or her" is the politically correct mode but in the fifties the possibility of attending university for a girl of working class background was statistically irrelevant. But girls had many other ways of filling the hiatus between school and finding a nice boy who would marry them: they could be typists, secretaries, receptionists, shop assistants, dressmakers, waitresses, nurses, for example. The world was their oyster – but here, the oyster is a metaphor for doors shut tight to prevent escape to a world of opportunities, so as to keep a girl, reverting to our earlier metaphor, on her railway lines heading to her predestined siding.

A special terror for pubescent girls in those far off days – the old ladies would shudder when they remembered it – was unprotected sex. The arrival of the contraceptive, not a moment too soon for these girls, was transformative. If you made a mistake, pre pill era, you had to rely on the boy doing the decent thing and marrying you.

Maureen had been recalling Jim and his telephone embarrassment while Angela and the others talked of George and how he now managed on his own, and what a nice girl his wife had been. 'Yous never can tell,' Brigitte said, and Jane and Angela nodded agreement. The "never can tell" must have referred to the unpredictability and unfairness with which death's icy hand strikes.

Maureen came out of her reverie. 'Let them enjoy themselves in the way they know how. They haven't much time left. Nor us for that matter. The time for change and new beginnings is long gone.'

'Er, what,' Angela asked.

'They know, or they think, we're self-sufficient without them. Our husbands I mean. Our children for the most part see us or communicate only out of their weak sense, very weak in these days, of filial obligation. We've done our turn as grandparents, the grandchildren are easily bored with us now they can work their laptops, tablets – whatever.'

Jane said: 'If I know our husbands, at this very moment they'll be yakking along similar cheery lines over their beers.'

Maureen's say was not over yet:

'There might have been a time. A time for a new beginning or something. But when someone jumps the gun either the race is started again immediately or it's let to go the full course; you don't call the runners back to start again when the finishing line is in sight.'

'And so...' Angela prompted.

'Our race is more than half over – much more, of course. At the end, the best you can do... God, Angela, what do I know? I'm a silly old eccentric woman. About to die, so the waiter thinks. What's my advice worth? But I know how I'm going to manage the rest of it; that at least. The rest of life with Jim, I mean.'

'How,' Jane asked, and the other two nodded to show they also wanted to know.

'When I was a teacher, one of the poems I had to bore my teenagers with was Arnold's *Dover Beach*. The last verse now means something special to me – Jim knows it too. What I get from it is the need for old people – old couples especially, for whom the future must become, sooner or later, grim, bleak, lonely, frightening even – the need for us to stick together. Better to go down among comrades than alone. I'm rambling: I've had too much to drink. It goes like this – the verse, if I *can* still remember it:

…Let us be true
To one another! For the world, which seems
To lie before us like a land of dreams,
So various, so beautiful, so new,
Hath really neither joy, nor love, nor light,
Nor certitude, nor peace, nor help for pain;
And we are here as on a darkling plain
Swept with confused alarms of struggle and flight,
Where ignorant armies clash by night.

'Thinking about it, though – changing my mind mid thought again! – What gets me most in the verse nowadays is not being old and on the "darkling plain". That's easy; we here – we're all better off than most people in the world; much better off; the "darkling plain" we can cope with. It's that the world never did seem, even when we were young, to "lie before us like a land of dreams". We missed out on that. So did our husbands. That's what gets me. It's what I feel cheated of.

'We were taught to have low expectations, to aim low – that we shouldn't even hope for the "various", the "beautiful", or the "new". Jim once told me that when he asked his teacher at his secondary modern school whether they would do A levels after their O levels, the teacher replied: "No – A levels are for the brighter children at Grammar schools; you, Anderton, should concentrate on woodwork, technical drawing and the like."'

Brigitte said: 'Well, despite everyzink we all done quite well, I zink.'

'It's the other way round nowadays,' Angela said; 'at school the kids are fed utterly unrealistic expectations about their future – even, or especially in fact, the academically challenged ones. Their slightest achievement is treated as if it was the latest piano sonata from the six-year old Mozart. They're all "brilliant" and everything they do is "brilliant" provided it isn't plain wrong or useless. "Brilliant" is the most over-used and inaccurately used epithet in schooling today.'

'I agree,' Maureen said, 'but how would you know, Angela?'

'Oh, I've substituted on parent days when my daughter and her husband couldn't attend and dutifully listened to my grandson's teachers. You know the drill: what he should pay extra attention to and all the other subjects in which – you've guessed it – he was *brilliant*.'

Jane's mobile began to play The Ride of the Valkyries loudly enough to make her friends laugh and other customers nearby look affronted.

'Andy set this bloody call tune,' Jane said, 'urgently rummaging through her handbag to answer and cut off the music. 'I don't know how to change it or even how to turn the volume down. Andy says he'll do it but I think he's no idea either.'

Relieved she found and silenced her mobile and, as if she had just extinguished a small fire, relaxed at a job well done in the nick of time.

'Hello. Yes, it's me, Jane. You Jim: me Jane. What are you phoning about, Jim; where's Andy?'

'It's Andy I'm phoning 'bout – about, I mean.'

'Christ, you sound drunk. What's going on? Where's Andy?'

'Andeez –,' Jim was on the verge of giving up the struggle to form words with mouth muscles that refused to respond. He remembered when his mouth had been prepared for multiple root canal treatment, and felt he had less control now. 'He's…'

'Put Andy on the phone, Jim, unless he's also too drunk to make sense. Christ! When are you guys gonna wake up to the fact that you're not teenagers any longer? Andy's not well enough to be getting drunk. Is he there?'

'I'll 'and y'over… Wins'on…'

Ten seconds of pub background noise supervened before the connection was broken.

155

Jane's first response was to look at her Samsung as if it had acted against her with malice aforethought. Then she said:

'Would you Adam and Eve it – would you bloody-well Adam and Eve it? That was Jim, Maureen, as you heard: drunk by the sound of it, as Andy no doubt is – all of them if one of them is. He phoned about Andy, then said he was handing the phone to Winston, then there was nothing but the background noise of whatever pub they're in. What are they up to, the clowns?'

Chapter 13

After Andy had knocked the remains of George's pint to the floor and been abused for his carelessness, he stood up in a peculiar way. He was leaning forwards with his hands on the table as if about to speak to a gathering of upwards of a hundred people; his eyes were making contact with imaginary audience participants at least half way to the back of a good-sized lecture hall.

'I feel jiggered…,' he said.

Then he added: 'As Dad used to say.'

Andy spoke in words audible only to his friends, despite his focus being still on the middle distance. Then, after a moment of suspense, he swayed and clasped the tabletop to steady himself, localising his focus while doing so. He saw that his friends were eyeing him with suspicion and fear. They could see, and could have confirmed without hesitation if required, that indeed he was jiggered – jiggered bad. They knew it was something more than drunkenness. Andy, however, merely wondered, vaguely curious, why they were looking at him in that strange way; it did not occur to him that he could have looked as bad as he felt. His complexion had never been fresh and virginal, not even when he was fresh and virginal, but now it was nightmarish, a Hammer Horror film back-from-the-tomb look.

Before anyone could respond to his 'I feel jiggered' symptom, Andy crumpled heavily in the direction he had only a moment ago sent George's pint. He lay on his back not attempting to get up and his eyes, though open, looked at nothing.

The atmosphere in the small bar soon became sombre; it was clear that whatever had happened to the old man on the floor was serious; it precluded simply carrying on drinking, laughing, talking about football, until the ambulance arrived. It was brought home to everyone that they were as insecure in a pub as anywhere else, despite the sense of sanctuary, of immunity that the interior of a pub usually gifts, and which is one of its chief attractions.

But before the sombre mood prevailed, pandemonium best describes the brief moments of frantic, almost comical activity following the general immediate appreciation that the man down was not going to get up under his own power. This was a situation; one that had to be dealt with promptly. Everyone had consumed alcohol to a greater or lesser extent, so everyone had an opinion and almost everyone uninhibitedly voiced it.

'Don't move him whatever you do!'

'Get him on his feet or turn him sideways – he'll swallow his tongue lying on his back.'

'Who said anything about moving him? Not me.'

'Somebody, like, give him the kiss of life, if yer know what I mean.'

'You do it, mate.'

An Irishman threw in his experience. 'Oi saw sumtink loik dis, meself, oi did, last Tursday 'appened in Sainsburys.'

'The Russians, was it?'

'Sainsburys, not Salisbury. Fockin 'ell!'

'He's breathing – look at him.'

'Is 'e a diabetic? I seen 'em go like that before. Funny stare they 'ave.'

'Yeah. Give 'im a biscuit or sumfin. Chocolate's good – the dark stuff.'

'Open a window – he needs air.'

'Poor bugger looks a goner to me.'

'Fella over there reckons the same thing happened last Thursday in Salisbury. The Russians, mate. We've probably all had our chips – the Nell could be cordoned off soon.'

'Must be in his seventies. Good way to go when you think about it. Croaking it with a pint in your hand.'

'P'raps he's just drunk.'

'That's not drunk. I know drunk when I see it.'

'Keep 'im warm; he needs a blanket over 'im.'

'Was he with you lot?' someone asked Andy's friends, who since his collapse had, in fact, being doing their best for him. Ben had ensured that the barmaid called for an ambulance. He was about to phone himself when he realised the state Andy was in, but Winston asked: 'Will the ambulance come to the Strand end or Maiden Lane end of Bull Inn Court?' (in which the Nell was situated), 'because the Court itself isn't accessible by motor traffic, I don't think.'

'The bar staff will know the drill,' Ben said. And George had folded a raincoat and put it under Andy's head for support, also because it seemed to him intrinsically wrong to leave a person's head lying on the bare floor of a pub. For his part, after the first minute or two, Jim agreed with his friends that Jane must be phoned and apprised of the situation.

'Okay, Jim, you'd better get on with it,' Winston said, 'but don't make it sound too bad; and tell her the ambulance is on its way. We hope!' George, while all this was going on, having done his good deed with the raincoat, was crouched beside the patient in the leapfrog position, looking stunned and contributing the comment, at regular intervals: 'He was fine a moment ago.'

Winston confirmed to the enquirer that Andy was indeed one of their party. Jim had taken a moment to pull himself together, and summon courage, prior to phoning Jane. 'Musn soun' drunk when I talk t'Jane. It'll give wrong impreshion…wrong idea.'

'Christ!' Winston said, overhearing Jim explain his plan.

Two ambulance men having arrived, the Nell customers immediately parted to create a path to Andy.

One of the medics stooped over the supine Andy and asked in a loud voice: 'Can you hear me? What's your name, mate?'

Whereupon, Winston said to Ben, out of the corner of his mouth, 'I hope he doesn't ask George because, at the moment, I'm not sure he could give the right answer, let alone poor old Andy. Look at him!'

'Who, George? Yeah, he looks like the stuffing's been knocked out of him,' Ben replied.

The story of the day was related to the medics while they got on with their procedures, which entailed exposing Andy's chest, taking various readings – the only ones which were obvious being the pulse and blood pressure, but wires were attached and bleeps came from a laptop-type machine. 'They're checking whether he's having a heart attack,' a pub "doctor" said confidently; then he downed his lager and let out a deep sigh, a sigh expressive of his sadness over there being no quietude, no escape from the hurly-burly to be found anywhere nowadays, not even in a pub.

Jim was now on his mobile. It had not started well; Thatcher-like tones assaulted his ears. He tried to recover control: 'It's Andy I'm phoning 'bout, Jane – about, I mean.'

Jim cringed at the response he got to his slurred information from the other end of the line. Winston and Ben could hear the strident, authoritative female voice, raised well above conversational volume, though the words were not clear enough to make out.

Jim had another go: 'Andeez...He's...'

The implacable female voice interrupted; it was louder still and the pace of delivery accelerated, and a stronger hectoring element thrown in. Jim crumbled under the verbal assault. He handed in his commission. 'I'll 'and y'over... Win'son,' was his parting comment to Jane.

In his haste to replace Winston in the firing line, Jim dropped the phone during handover. It went under the table. In their eagerness to retrieve it, Winston and Ben both bent double at the same moment and crashed heads together with such force that Winston staggered and sat back on the floor dazed and disorientated. Ben took the blow like the old boxer of legend that he was – though it triggered a message from his bladder, and he was off to the basement as fast as he could push a way through the spectators. 'Back in a minute.'

Jim was glad to discover, when he retrieved his phone, that the connection was lost. He had meekly, fearfully spoken into it, hoping for failure: 'Jane, you still there?' Then: 'Is dead, the phone.'

George looked angrily at Jim. 'For Christ's sake, Jim, phone again. She's got to know what's going on.'

Jim, surprised, answered, 'Oh, you back in the land of the living, George, are you?'

No one was taking any notice of Winston – the main points of interest being still Andy and Jim's phone call – but he was back on his feet and looking at his sorry image in the large mirror over the fireplace. He was dabbing pocket tissues at blood streaming from his forehead. 'Jesus, what's Angela going to say when she sees this,' he kept muttering during efforts to staunch the flow; a task made delicate and difficult because bits of tissue paper kept sticking to the wound.

Jim had done his duty and phoned Jane again but as soon as he heard Jane's 'What's going on, Jim, just tell me?' one of the ambulance men began firing questions at him about Andy. George was with the fairies again – he was sitting at the table now but looking shattered and far too introspective given the situation. Winston was preoccupied at the mirror; Ben, as usual, was in the lavatory. Jim had a brainwave – a cowardly brainwave. 'Don't worry, Jane, Andy's c'llapsed – prob'ly had one over th'eight – the amb'lance team – they're sorting him out now. Best you talk direct to guy. He'll fill you in.' With that, which of course left Jane terrified, Jim gave the phone to the ambulance man and explained – looking as if he was having a stroke while doing so: 'His swife – Andy swife – told her what's happened – give her the gen. Better you do it; she'll want t'know where you're taking him, and so on.'

Ben reappeared, heard the tail-end of Jim's telephone conversation, and offered to go with Andy in the ambulance.

The mood at the wives' table reflected devastation at the news as they pieced together what had happened from Jane's conversation with the ambulance man, which concluded:

'So Ben – Mr Walker that is – is going with you in the ambulance, you say?' Jane said.

'Yes, if that's okay with you, Mrs Patton. He's offered.'

'Fine. I'll get a taxi direct to the hospital if you could tell Mr Walker, please.'

'I'll get the restaurant to get a taxi,' said Maureen, and she got up and spoke to their ever-willing waiter.

Jane was quiet and pensive after her phone call, taking time to digest the bad news and its implications. Angela and Brigitte offered their sympathy and made various suggestions, but the first concrete action came from Angela:

'I'll settle the bill so we're ready to go; we can sort out the detail later.'

Maureen said that she would go with Jane in the taxi, and she did so in a manner that made refusal obviously a futile prospect. The party broke up and said their goodbyes in a fraught and emotional state. Between the kisses and hugs, support and concern were expressed; Jane had to assure everyone that she would pass on any news as soon as she received it. When Jane and Maureen left for their taxi, the others each immediately phoned their husbands. Jane and Maureen looked ashen.

In the ambulance, medicated and comfortable, with Ben accompanying him, Andy felt calm, almost untroubled, tranquil, despite his awareness that something serious had occurred, and occurred to him exclusively.

'Probably a heart attack,' he mumbled, lying on his back turning over in his mind what he could remember of the events of the last half an hour – which was not much. 'There was terrible pain,' he said aloud, though unaware that he was talking, not merely thinking: 'bad pain.'

Ben heard this and tried to reassure his friend. 'It's okay now, Andy, we'll be at the hospital soon. They'll sort you out.' Whether Andy heard could not be ascertained; he continued his own train of thought: 'It was my chest and arm, I think. Still feel tight in the chest.'

Andy knew he had not been conscious continuously since whatever had happened to him happened. He could recall lying on the floor of the Nell and not knowing why he was there, and he knew he had been in pain because when he thought about his time on the floor he felt a vestige of the panic which the pain had caused him; it was a panic he had experienced once when he broke a leg years ago and suffered agonising pain. But now he was grateful to be in an ambulance being taken care of. He comforted himself with the thought that the old NHS might not be able to stop him dying but at least they could be relied on to prevent him from feeling intolerable pain. 'If this is what the end is like,' he mumbled, inaudibly this time, 'then it's not too bad – not too bad.' Audibly, he suddenly said, 'P'raps I'm diabetic – maybe that's it.'

'Could be, Andy,' Ben said, trying to put the best gloss on things.

Andy drifted into sleep – very willingly too. He was thinking, while he let himself go, that it would be nice to wake up and find he was recovering from whatever had happened to him, but, conversely, that he could not resist the drift into sleep whatever – 'No, not even if they told me I'd never wake up again… I've had a good innings anyway. Nothing's going to get better. What's to struggle for?'

His sleep was pleasant and dream-filled. Recollections of happy days followed one upon another in dreams of childhood. Then his idyllic world was violated by bleeping sounds, and he thought he ought to wake up and investigate, but he could not be bothered. He wanted to finish this last dream. *That will be enough,* he thought – *that will be enough for one ordinary bloke's life.* He shut out the sound of bleeping.

In this last dream he was back in Shernhall Street in his childhood home, sitting opposite dad at the fireplace; they were both keeping stock-still. They were waiting for the mice to venture out so that dad – now immobile as the Sphinx but dressed for relaxation in his gardening trousers and collarless white shirt (a red mark showing at the base of his neck where the collar studs pained him) – so that dad could whack the vermin with the fire poker and, as he put it, 'keep on top o' the buggers.' Population control was his goal; he accepted that elimination was a pipe dream.

Andy's dream then took a turn which surprised him, surprised him even in his dream. His dad, a man normally determined to the point of obsession when in pursuit of mice, said to him, 'Let's forget about catching the mice tonight, Andy lad. Live and let live, hey. We'll 'ave a good talk together instead – Mum too.' He looked wistful and, upsetting for Andy, a bit sad before broaching his chosen topic. He looked at Andy in his always kindly, cherishing way and said, 'We did 'ave a good time at Butlin's in Minehead that year, didn't we? – D'you still remember it Andy, like I do? You were – what? – only six or seven then, I s'pose.'

'Yes, it was good, Dad. Smashing! The best.' Andy meant it too. It gave him a jolt in his dream, a twitch that Ben noticed, to hear himself using that word of childhood again – 'Smashing!'

The last thing said by Andy in the ambulance, just audible to Ben, was, 'Tell Jane…happens to everyone…it's okay; and love and thanks. KBO.'

The last thought Andy had before death was, *Yes, I once had a smashing time, the best: my own smashing time that no one else ever had or will have: on the beach at Minehead. Can't ask for more.* And he felt that the smashing time was still there.

Andy lay there, after the medics had gone through their efforts to resuscitate – fleshy, pasty-faced, pock-marked, overweight; but he went to wherever it was – who knows? – happily confident that he would always be the apple of his dad's eye.

'Jesus Effing Christ!' Ben said, amazed and half disbelieving when the medics explained why they were giving up. Basically, they were out of time. Andy had been dead for long enough to make further effort, which Ben urged on them, pointless.

Ben, after cursory enquiries about 'what next?', 'how long before we get to the hospital?' – sent a text to Jim telling him that Andy had died in the ambulance, and that it seemed certain it was a heart attack.

In the Nell, Jim, Winston and George were dithering over what they should be doing…would it be right simply to go home their separate ways and, as the news bulletins have it, await further developments? Of course, only after texting their wives as to what had befallen Andy – namely, his collapse and remove to hospital. The alternative, soon dismissed, was to stay in the Nell together until Ben sent news. A couple of texts had gone off before Ben's notification of death came through. Jim, feeling clear-headed now but physically pretty awful, looked Winston and George in the eye and said, 'That's it for our Andy, boys – Ben says he died in the ambulance. Heart attack.'

'So Jane's going to the hospital to rendezvous with the corpse of her husband,' Winston said. His blinking albino eyes suited, for once, the sinister subject matter. 'Bloody hell! What a rotten way for it to happen – for her, I mean.'

'I'll be back in a minute,' George said, moving off, to aunty's presumably.

'We talked earlier today – God, it seems an age ago now – about us all going out with a bang; do you remember?' Jim asked Winston.

'Of course. Case of tempting fate, I suppose. It's funny, but since we met this morning I've had the feeling that today was unusual, that something out of the ordinary was going to happen.'

'Whatever it was, another old mate's gone. No more taxi driver stories… I met Andy's parents once, in another century so it seems now; his dad idolised him, and vice versa I got the impression.'

'It's selfish to say it, but it's not just Andy who's died: it's a part of our lives that's now dead and gone, Jim, with him. You know what I mean, I'm sure.'

'No man is an island, and all that,' Jim said by way of agreement. 'How does it go? "Any man's death diminishes me, because I am involved in mankind." His death diminishes us for sure; Andy wasn't just any man – not in our lives.'

'Oops. That's mine,' Winston said, retrieving his ringing and vibrating phone. 'Hello. Yes, Angela. Yes… Yes… Well, yes, a few drinks but not drinking-for-England as you put it, dear… Look, Angela – wait a moment – that's academic now – things have moved on; Andy's dead… Christ, give us a break – I didn't kill him, you know… It was a heart attack – in the ambulance… Well – look – I *couldn't* tell you earlier, that's why; we've only just heard ourselves, from Ben… I agree, then you ought to text Maureen, so she can break it to Jane… Okay… yes, bloody awful… Yep, bye for now. We're all making our way home.'

'Angela giving you a rough time?'

'Yes.'

'Well, it doesn't look great, does it? He had a medical condition, and he got drunk with us and had a heart attack. What's with Maureen breaking it to her?'

'She's with Jane on the way to the hospital.'

'Oh. What hospital is it anyway?'

'Buggered if I can remember. They did say. Will they just take him to any hospital now he's dead – any hospital with a mortuary?'

'Where's George? We ought to be packing up now.'

'I need to go to aunty's first. P'raps he's snuffed it sitting on the bog. Two down three to go. Agatha Christie's writing today's script, Jim, I think.'

They both laughed and it relieved the tension. Winston then went off on the perilous journey to the centre of the earth. Jim sat looking glum, the laugh was soon over.

When Winston came back a few minutes later, breathless, and Jim caught sight of him, he saw that Winston was anxious. George was not in aunty's.

'He's not down there,' Winston confirmed. 'Where the hell *is* he?'

Jim shrugged his shoulders. 'He's been – I don't know – peculiar today: not consistent. One minute he's on the ball, next he's vague as hell.'

'Gone home without telling us – just forgot. It's possible, with the shock of Andy's death and all that. Worrying all the same.'

'That must be it,' Jim agreed, in want of any other explanation.

Chapter 14

Jane and Maureen arrived at the hospital before Andy's ambulance. By then they were already aware that he was dead. Maureen had received Angela's text while Andy's ambulance was still rattling along and Maureen and Jane were still in their taxi. Maureen had thought it best to break the news to Jane immediately. The two of them entered the hospital's reception area shocked, tearful and at a loss what to do next – a common enough experience among hospital visitors. It was not long before a demented-looking Ben arrived; the first thought of the two ladies on seeing him, though, was that Andy's ambulance was just outside reception.

Ben ran into the reception area and quickly came face to face with Jane and Maureen. Inarticulate, for whatever reason – drink, grief, anger? – He gave vent to his thoughts and feelings by waving his arms and pulling faces expressive of his torture. In his tormented state he embraced Jane first and then Maureen; the latter, if he had thought about it, only so as not to let her feel left out. On a sudden, as if realising he had made the wrong decision, he cut short his embrace with Maureen and ran off down a corridor. The old ladies did not guess why; how were they to know he had not been to aunty's in a while? And there was no aunty's in the reception area.

Having no luck in the long corridor he had chosen at random – all the doors were signed for staff, consultants of various descriptions, or simply as private, or no access – Ben chanced a left turn at the end and collided with a trolley coming towards him, one laden with equipment, being pushed by a female of sumo proportions.

'Christ!' he yelled, bouncing off, 'why are all nurses so bloody enormous? – you're in the bloody health service, after all.'

'Who the fuck you think you're talking too, and what you doin' runnin' dis way, mister?'

There was equipment lying on the floor. Ben dimly sensed he had gone too far. He was utterly desperate for aunty's, so he decided to run on in search of relief. By way of excuse for abandoning the scene without effort at amends, he yelled: 'Aunty's – need aunty's,' and ran off in the direction of what turned out to be Paediatrics.

The infuriated trolley pusher alerted security to her sighting of a maniac heading at speed for Paediatrics – 'Drunk or high on something,' she said, 'shaven-headed and with a broken nose.'

Ben was standing at a urinal in the aunty's he found close by the entrance to the Paediatrics Centre, beginning to feel much better and that God was in his heaven and all right with the world (Andy's death forgotten for the moment) when two brawny security men burst in, one of whom confidently announced into his talkie: 'We've got him – he's skulking in the lavatory outside Paediatrics. We can take care of him. We'll bring him to room X via J lift – be there in a couple of minutes.'

Ben had finished and zipped up when it dawned on him what the security men were doing, and that it was he who had been described as skulking in the lavatory. He had no time to think. One of the men said to him, obviously trying to be conciliatory but equally obviously determined to be obeyed: 'We'd like you to come with us without any trouble, sir, so we can talk upstairs.' The two men stood arms akimbo with thumbs inside the belts of their uniforms.

Ben had recently become adept at summoning up the old red mist, and today he was on form. His boxing ducking and diving skills enabled him to evade the clutches of the two large men, both encumbered with the paraphernalia of their profession; and once he was out of aunty's he darted back along the corridor that had led him towards Paediatrics.

When he reached reception again, travelling at a great lick, he caught sight of Jane and Maureen and bawled as he ran past in the direction of the main entrance:

'Security after me... Pervert...! Me...? Christ!'

'What in God's name is going on?' an astonished Maureen asked. 'Where is he off to and what was he talking about? Why would security...'

The question died on her lips when she saw security men lope past and heard a member of staff at reception shout: 'The beast went that way – through the entrance doors. He looked just the type.'

It was raining hard now, and in front of the A and E reception area several ambulances were disburdening their catch from a serious road accident that had occurred locally within the half hour. Police cars were also arriving. Into this melee ran Ben, beginning now to stagger from exhaustion. Seeing police cars arrive spooked him, sent him over the top. 'What's happening to me?' he asked himself. 'I used to be a Lloyd's underwriter – deputy anyway.'

He saw a gap between two ambulances and through the gap a clear way to the main road and freedom across a patch of green. Summoning up the blood, he ran for it. There was an enormous thud. A police car on the far side of the ambulances had accelerated in response to an order to return to the accident scene as soon as possible; it was passing the gap between the two ambulances when Ben ran through it. The last thing Ben experienced in this world was surprise at finding himself looking down, very briefly, at a police car passing beneath him. He had felt no pain and quickly felt nothing anymore.

'What was that great bang?' asked Jane, shaken by it out of a stupor.

'Search me, Jane,' Maureen answered; 'what happens at A and E nowadays is anybody's business… And where's Ben now, I wonder.'

The conversation was interrupted and ended when Jane was invited to accompany a white-coated woman to a room close by, presumably to hear something, all that the hospital deemed she should know, about the demise of her husband: files have to be closed.

Back at the Nell, the atmosphere had returned to normal; the collapse and stretching away of a customer had a short life of interest among its customers. Jim and Winston had tried to get in touch with George – still mysteriously vanished – by phone, but without success. They sent a text but got no reply to that either before they decided to leave; leave saddened by the drift of things during a day that had begun well, to make their separate ways home. To both of them the journey loomed ominously; they were tired, whether by the day's exertions or by life itself; of which, it occurred to them both, perhaps they had had their fill by now.

'Well, Winston, old friend, take care. We'll talk about all this, I dare say, tonight, tomorrow or whenever.'

'Yep. Look after yourself Jim,' Winston replied, as though they were parting for a very long time, each with a perilous mission ahead of him; 'not many of us left now.'

'Ben must be having a rough time with Jane and Maureen. Rather him than me.'

'Yep.'

'Bye anyway, old friend.'

'Bye Jim.'

The haggard old men separated; "old geezers" would not have been an appropriate description of them now as they made off in opposite directions along the Strand. An old geezer – especially a diamond old geezer – has vitality, can still surprise, still looks as if he has a stake in the world, can be feisty on occasion, capable of chutzpah. Jim and Winston, despite wishing each other well on parting company, both felt it was high time their brief candle was blown out. They had strutted and fretted their hour upon the stage – mostly fretted; curtain time had come.

And what of George? An old man with a shock of white hair and much loose skin hanging in folds and creases on his expressionless face was sitting on a bus, upstairs, which was going down Hackney Road in the direction of Mare Street and Clapton. He felt tired, confused and vaguely insecure. He knew where he was – it was familiar of old – but not why he was there, what was his destination, his purpose in the journey. He thought he must have forgotten – he believed he must have known when he caught the bus but had since forgotten; after all, he had had a lot to drink.

'Where do I get off?' he asked himself out loud, surprising himself with the sound of his own voice. He must have looked bad. Another passenger said:

'Where are you wanting to get to, mate?' This embarrassed George. He could think of no answer, except to say in reply, which he did:

'It's okay, thanks.' The passenger looked at him doubtfully and said:

'Suit yourself, mate'.

At the bottom of Hackney Road, the bus turned left into Mare Street, and George was disturbed to see so many new buildings, or, at least, buildings new to him. It must have been twenty years since he last passed this way, which a long time ago was his daily route to and from the Minster Insurance Company. The first place he looked out for, on the right, was the Essoldo cinema which he and Tony Turner used to visit weekly, but it was gone, probably long gone, and George was not even sure that he could identify the building; very disappointing.

Of course, the large and imposing Hackney Town Hall, which soon came up on his left, set well back from the road – that he not only remembered well but had often seen on television down the years. Hackney contrived to produce more than its share of political, social, and economic news stories, many with a hint of scandal in them to ensure their newsworthiness; and Hackney Town Hall was the backdrop which television reporters invariably used for their story to camera. The indomitable Hackney Empire was still there, too, which gave George a lift; he had been on its stage once singing Christmas carols in the school choir.

Approaching the railway bridge, beyond which was Hackney Tower and the "Narrow Way", George looked at where Woolworths once throve, and fondly remembered its woodblock flooring and the heavy wooden counters that made up the rectangular islands of different merchandise. The broken biscuit island was his favourite as a child; you could make up your own selection from innumerable square metal tins of damaged biscuits, shovelling biscuits into a paper bag and then paying on the weight. Most mothers would know by experience how many ounces they had collected before the scales settled.

'*I* remember,' George said, surprised again to hear it out loud – 'I remember it, but who the fuck cares anymore?' Passengers began to keep a wary eye on him.

They were relieved when they saw him going downstairs preparing to get off at the stop just under the bridge on the left, still located outside the premises that he would always remember as Gibbons, the furniture store – but which was now – *God knows what!* – He was not able to make out.

In the fresh cold air, a hint of rain about still, George looked around. He was frightened; he knew precisely where he was, but he had no idea why he had come there. He lived elsewhere and had done for decades. It was as if he had been transported back to his childhood – there was a dreamlike quality to his experience; it felt to him that he might be imagining he was there – but he could not break the spell. As when he was a child, he was aware that if he had wanted to talk to the people around him in the street, he would not have known where to begin. Something was wrong with him, he knew – but what? Beginning to feel desperate, he forced himself to reconstruct in his mind the events of his day: to get a grip.

What George was able to bring to mind relating to the past half day was episodic and did not fit into any time sequence, any narrative, that made sense and which could explain his presence, here and now, standing in St John's churchyard looking up at Hackney Tower – at some point since his time, so he discovered from reading the plaque, renamed St Augustine's Tower.

I must go home, he thought with great relief, sure he had found the answer – *that's it, just go home and rest and then everything will begin to make sense. Must make sense or I'm done for.* It frightened him that he was trembling unaccountably. 'Can't be the bloody DT's, surely. I'm not an alcoholic, am I?' he shouted at the rain and sky.

It was then that he began to feel that panic might overwhelm him; he could not remember where he lived! He could picture his home in his mind, no problem – his garden, his neighbours, the corner shop – but where was it, his home? It was not in Clapton anymore, and had not been for ages; but where *was* it? 'Where *is* it? What train station do I use?' he yelled. He had forgotten about his mobile phone, so it did not occur to him to phone a friend for help. He decided to find a coffee bar and have a strong coffee and a rest, in the hope that the two together would sort him out.

A large Americano in front of him, George sat looking out of the window. Nothing caught his eye. Because there was not much going on in his head his gaze no more took in what it rested upon than the beam of a lighthouse registers passing ships.

George sat over his coffee for half an hour, but if told he had sat there for three hours or five minutes it would have been all the same to him. When, eventually, he did feel it was time to make a move – though where to, he dared not think about – he took out his wallet intending to pay, becoming aware as he did so that something had dropped to the floor. A cursory look failed to find anything; he was not focussing well, what with the drink and whatever else was happening to him. He took a fiver out of his wallet and went to the counter; of course, he was told he had already paid on ordering. He left confused and embarrassed, and still with no idea what he was doing, where he should be going, or even, he sensed but could not face, a clear one of who he was.

'I'm George Rodgers,' he said to himself, walking aimlessly. 'One of Mrs Beamish's breakfasts would sort me out, I reckon.' Then he added, recalling those happy days: 'Though I was never a Drayton.' George laughed out loud at the memory. Then he was down in the dumps again. He desperately sought some point of reference, any point of reference. *I used to work – where? – At Minster, of course. Then there was my own business, but when did that start?*

'Christ!' he shouted, 'What's happening to me?' It reassured him to see Hackney Baths coming into view. 'All the happy hours I spent there learning to swim.' George began talking aloud all the time now. 'Males and females had separate pools in those days – I remember that much.'

Because he did not know where he was going – had no destination of any kind in mind, no objective – George kept walking. He sensed he would remain calmer, more collected, walking than he would be if he found somewhere to sit down and – and think. Thinking was difficult at the moment and walking occupied the mind. Perhaps he hoped – unconsciously that is – that his legs knew where he ought to be going.

Whether by chance or hidden design, it was not long before these old legs brought him to the top of Powerscroft Road; he was walking along Lower Clapton Road in the direction of Lea Bridge Road. There, large as life, on the right, was the Round Chapel; and it was unchanged, the place where he had been to cubs and scouts as a child and youngster. But what now?

Powerscroft Road was where George had lived out his childhood – but what of that? Why was he standing there now, looking down it as he passed along Lower Clapton Road, having left it nigh on fifty years ago? These thoughts were soon superseded in his addled mind; sustained thinking – two linked consecutive thoughts, for example – was rapidly on the way out. It suddenly dawned on him – from seeing every pedestrian around him talking into their mobiles, wherever he walked – that he had a phone. 'I'll phone Winston… Winston will know what to do. Winston always has an answer.' That sequence of thoughts, spoken aloud, stretched his cognitive powers to their limit.

Then he pulled the trigger that shot him through with overwhelming panic – fear and animal panic: his mobile was missing, though he rummaged frantically many times in every pocket he could find. Given his crazy state – self-confidence at its lowest point; non-existent for all practical purposes – it is not surprising that he began to doubt ever having had a mobile. Things, as they sometimes do when already bad, then took a turn for the worse

'Ye gods! My wallet – where is it? Gone, Christ! Gone. Gone with my bloody phone! It's got to be a nightmare, a practical joke. Please, God, let me not be mad,' George cried, dimly aware that his words were familiar but far from recalling them as once used by King Lear at a similar low point in his fortunes.

Only once in his life had George felt fear and panic as he did now; the fear and panic that makes people jump screaming out of the twentieth floor of a burning skyscraper. It was when he was on holiday in the West Country all those years ago with Winston and Jim. The three of them found a quiet bay and decided to have a swim; it was sunny and warm and the water looked calm – what could go wrong? Nothing until they decided they had had enough and would return to the sandy beach from where they were, some fifty to a hundred yards out. They had not noticed the danger flag on one side of the bay, there to deter swimming at critical times when tidal movements created a powerful undertow. It had not even occurred to the lads that such warnings might ever be given.

By chance, Winston and Jim escaped the strongest part of the undercurrent but, nevertheless, emerged from the sea tired enough to be glad they were out of it. George experienced the undertow at its most powerful. Immediately he struck for land, he knew he was not making any progress; worse, he saw and felt that he was drifting further out despite swimming as hard as he could. He felt panic such as he had never experienced before and put every ounce of energy into his swimming; panic made him swim more strongly than he would have believed possible of himself. When he got to the beach, utterly exhausted, he flopped on his front gasping for breath. For several minutes he was incapable of speech and of answering the questions fired at him by Winston and Jim, though he could see that they regarded the episode as a great joke.

'Those were the days,' George said, smiling broadly as he wandered to and fro along Lower Clapton Road, every now and then, when he reached the junction with Powerscroft Road, looking at the Round Chapel across the way. Paradoxically, his panic was in remission for the moment thanks to recollections of his earlier experience of blind panic.

An hour later, George's increasingly eccentric and erratic behaviour, coupled with his old age, led to his being dealt with by the authorities. Someone must have stopped and watched George for a few minutes and contacted the emergency services to notify them that an old man needed to be taken in hand. George's age would have been the deciding factor. No one nowadays bats an eyelid at finding a *young* person sitting alone on a bench roaring with laughter, or yelling angrily, simultaneously gesticulating violently, rocking back and forth – it is generously assumed that they are communicating via social media. An old man behaving in an identical manner, however, is judged as gaga, and white coats are called in to remove the threat.

The white coats were justified, in fairness, in George's case. He was unable to account coherently for his day, or explain his intentions for the rest of it, or inform the white coats of his place of habitation, or even, towards the end of their interrogation, tell them his name with any conviction. 'Er, George it is – yes, George, that's it.' His having no form of identification about his person sealed the deal so far as the white coats were concerned.

In a van on the way to somewhere, all George could think about – it did not cross his mind to ask where he was being taken – was a pleasant middle-aged waitress who worked at El Vino's in Fleet Street and whose jolly and friendly character was reason enough for lunching there. 'Those were the days,' George said, winking at one of the white coats, who nodded in agreement though having no idea what George was referring to. And for his part, George had no idea that he was talking about the afternoon of this fateful day, on which he had lost his mind. He suddenly felt profoundly tired and fell gratefully into deep sleep, all sense of panic and anxiety vanished now that kind people were looking after him.

Chapter 15

When Jim and Winston went their separate ways in the Strand, neither knew of Ben's tragic death. And neither suspected that George's mind had gone – how could they, despite Winston having had an uneasy feeling about him all day? It was not long, however, before each received a phone from his wife:

'Winston,' Angela said, 'more bad news, I'm afraid – very bad.'

'What, for God's sake, Angela? Just tell me.'

'It's Ben – he's dead. I'm sorry.'

'Andy you mean – Ben was in the ambulance with him. And anyway, we know about Andy; we heard from Ben. You're behind the curve, dear; I know it's been hectic.'

'Bloody listen, Winston: we know Andy is dead. But now, Ben is dead too. He ran in front of a police car after being chased out of the hospital by security staff. They thought he was some sort of crazed paedophile. Maureen phoned me and I had to break the news to Brigitte.'

All Winston could say was, 'Paedophile – Ben? Why?' And without waiting for an answer, 'You didn't tell Brigitte that story, I hope. Christ!'

'Apparently he was found skulking in the lavatory outside Paediatrics. And, no, I didn't put it like that to Brigitte. Who do you think I am: you?'

Winston screamed: 'HE'S ALWAYS IN THE LAVATORY. HE HAS A CONDITION!'

'Yes, *I* know that, Winston – no point shouting at me – but they didn't.'

'So – let me get this straight – they chased the poor old devil out of the hospital and he ran in panic in front of a police car and was killed. Was it instant?'

'I gather it was, thank heaven.'

'"Thank heaven"! What do you mean – "thank heaven"? They as good as murdered him.'

'It's awful, I know, but it'll take time to sort out. Whatever *we* may know about Ben, tomorrow's local paper is going to be leading on the escaping paedophile who got his comeuppance.'

Winston had been sitting on the cold and still damp retaining wall of a fountain in Trafalgar Square when he took Angela's call – just resting. Hearing her preview of tomorrow's local newspaper headlines, he began to laugh, helplessly. When he regained sufficient self-control, he said out loud:

'Two down, three to go!' Then: 'Is this the promised end? All of us going out with a bang together?'

After these questions, a hysterical note characterised his continuous raucous laughter. A girl who passed by said to him in a friendly way, 'You've had a good day by the sound of it.'

'Good day? Oh, yes – you don't know the half of it. Absolutely spiffing. We won't see the like of it again: two of us won't, that's for sure.'

There was something unsettling in the elderly albino's manner – the way he blinked, perhaps – that made the girl decide to avoid further conversation and accelerate her pace.

Jim got a phone call from Maureen when he was limping down Fleet Street in the direction of Ludgate Circus.

'Hello, dear,' he said, seeing that the call was from his wife. 'Terrible news about Andy, isn't it?'

'Yes, but that's not all, Jim. There's more bad news.'

'More bad news. What's bad news compared to one of your oldest friends suddenly dying on you?'

'Another one dying, Jim – that would fit the bill, wouldn't it?' Maureen said this with the intention of preparing Jim for the shock.

'Well, I've been with Winston and George until a short while ago, and Ben was in the ambulance with Andy, so you'll have seen him at the hospital, I should think. So what are you talking about, Maureen? It's been a long day: put me in the picture.'

Cutting to the chase, Maureen said: 'I'm sorry to say that Ben is dead.'

'But Andy's dead; how can Ben be dead? He was in the ambulance with Andy. It was Ben who told us Andy'd died.'

'It's a long story, but Ben was knocked down and killed by a police car outside the hospital.'

'But how? How could that happen?'

Jim heard Maureen take in a deep breath before replying:

'He was running out of the hospital to escape security staff who were convinced he was a paedophile –'

'Paedophile!'

'Yes, Jim. Paedophile. Two security men discovered him. Skulking in the gents, they said, next to the Paediatrics ward – that was after a nurse alerted them he'd run past her going in that direction. Then once outside the hospital, trying to make his escape, it seems Ben ran between two parked ambulances just as a police car was accelerating past them on the other side.'

'Jesus! And George has gone AWOL. That only leaves me and Winston who can be accounted for.'

'George gone AWOL?'

'Blimey! What a day this is turning out to be. It solves Ben's marital problems, I suppose. Ironic, you'd have to say.'

'The irony wasn't something I'd thought about, Jim.'

'Why do we worry about anything? Life sorts us all out if we give it time. Quite frankly, Maureen – You still there?'

'Yes, Jim, still listening.'

'Quite frankly… Oh, it doesn't matter. It's just that I've had enough now, myself. I wouldn't want you getting upset if I snuffed it. We're all old; it's time. Ben – a paedophile – it's insane!'

'Well, I suggest you take a different line, Jim, if you find yourself talking to Jane or Brigitte. I mean about it being time to go. Me – I can take it. The paedophile nonsense will get sorted, I dare say.'

'Ben – Ben a paedophile? Why, for Christ's sake, did anyone get that idea?'

'I suppose that's not important now. Anyway, I'd better finish, battery's running low. Take care on the way home.'

Back in Trafalgar Square Winston was setting off in the direction of Charing Cross for Leicester Square underground. He was a conspicuous figure, wavy blond hair – remnants of it – red blotchy face, expensively dressed, and he had forgotten to put his top of the range mobile back into his pocket; he was holding it loosely in his right hand as he walked at a moderate stagger along the pavement. He was preoccupied with the events of the day, but after a couple seconds his brain responded to the sound of a motor cycle or scooter behind him; it appeared to be getting too close for safety.

Looking round he had no time to react to a scooter which came close enough to make him fall over, drop his mobile, but not to injure him. The rider's identity was hidden by his helmet and face mask. He picked up Winston's mobile from the pavement and was on the point of making his getaway when Winston grabbed his leg. The rider instantly squirted something at Winston from a container in his right hand, but he was off balance and whatever the substance was it went over Winston's back. Winston realised what was happening – guessed he was being attacked with acid – and threw his weight at the scooter and its rider, taking care not to raise his face and make it an easy target. The scooter toppled and its rider fell badly, yelping in pain when he hit the road. Winston was over him in a second and kicked him hard in the back, repeatedly. After about a minute, Winston by then tiring of the kicking, the dazed youngster began struggling to get to his feet. A couple of bystanders intervened to separate them, but it was not until a police car arrived – very soon – and two policemen hauled Winston from the scooter rider, who was still on all fours, that the fracas was ended.

In the police station an exhausted Winston found himself being interrogated over his response to being knocked down, having his phone stolen, and acid squirted over him. It seems the boy scooter rider, a fifteen-year-old, had suffered a couple of broken ribs; whether from his fall or Winston's kicking was not yet known, if it ever would be.

'That'll teach him a lesson,' Winston said on hearing about the boy's injury, fully expecting the police interviewer to nod vigorously in agreement.

Instead, his interviewer answered:

'That may very well be the case, sir, but what concerns us is whether reasonable force was used by you to deter your attacker, a juvenile.'

Winston looked apoplectic.

'Why were you kicking the boy when he was lying on the ground,' the interviewer asked, taking no notice of Winston's expression of outrage.

'In the first place, I didn't know he was a boy – he was big enough to have been an adult. Secondly, he had attacked me, and though he fell with his bike into the road, *after* stealing my mobile, there was no reason for me to believe he wouldn't carry on with his attack, and his attempt at theft, when he got up again. So, while he was down, I made bloody sure that when he next got up he wouldn't be in any condition to attack me – me, an old man, in case you haven't noticed.'

'You admit, then, that you attacked him, kicked him, when he was lying on the ground – in the road, from our records – having fallen over with his scooter? That is, when he was no longer posing a threat to you?'

'I thought he'd be a threat again if I let him get up and waited for him to make up his mind what was the best way for him to spend the rest of his day; let's put it that way.'

All hell suddenly broke out in the station. (For some reason, it only now occurred to Winston that he did not know which police station he was in.) Policemen began to appear from nowhere and ran furiously along corridors. Winston's interview was brought to a close. When his interviewer had popped his head out of the door of their little room and made some enquiries, he turned to Winston and said: 'Seems there's been a shooting in the Farringdon Street area. Could be terror-related. Obviously, sir, our talk is on the back burner for the time being; I'm going to be otherwise engaged. The station staff will look after you – do you want a coffee?'

Declining police hospitality, Winston sat back to review his day in the warmth and quiet of the interview room.

A few hours ago we were all in the Farringdon Street area, he reflected. *Not so much a case of what a difference a day makes,* he thought, laughing mirthlessly and blinking unnecessarily, *as what a difference a few hours can make.* The blotches that characterised the skin on his face were distinctly mauve now. Being alone Winston now gave voice to his thoughts:

'A few hours ago, we five life-long friends met for lunch, as we have done so often down the years; since then, two of us have died, one of whom was chased to his death as a suspected paedophile; I've been attacked and am being held for questioning on some kind of assault charge; and a terrorist incident is

181

currently taking place in the street we all met in earlier – where, incidentally, we were kicked out of the pub because of a bomb scare; oh, and one of us, dear old George, has vanished into thin air – about which I fear the worst. Christ all bleeding mighty! I feel pretty buggered up myself. Should I phone Angela and tell her I'm in the clink for kicking a fifteen-year-old nearly to death? I think not. Let's see what transpires – the world can't really be as mad as it's been behaving lately.'

Winston turned to thinking about George and what might have caused his disappearance. Deep down he feared that there was some issue about George's mental condition – dementia or the like; he could not believe George would up and go without saying anything, not when he was normal. And even today, Winston remembered, he had been disconcerted once or twice by odd, uncharacteristic behaviour from George.

We will know soon enough, he thought. Then he got up with every intention, now that things were again calm in the station – 'All quiet on the western front,' he said to himself – of leaving his room in search of that coffee. But once upright, he felt frighteningly stiff in all his joints. Worse still, he was dizzy. His head swam as if he were swinging it around rather than standing still, and he became aware of a rhythmical thumping which he soon diagnosed as a severe pounding pain in his head. He wanted to sit down, but he felt so stiff he doubted he could do it. Within a couple of seconds the decision took itself: he fell into his seat and his head, now that he was unconscious, tipped backwards over the top of the chair at an ungainly angle. His eyes remained open.

Over in the Farringdon Street area – the locus of the incident which terminated Winston's police interview – the situation was under control. An area had been cordoned off, traffic diverted, television cameras and reporters were on the scene, and half a dozen police cars were parked within twenty yards of the killings, of which there had been three. The police had already established the essentials of the incident. It was not terrorism but a gangland dispute that had resulted in the tragic death of an innocent bystander, a male, as well as two known gang members. Witnesses confirmed that the elderly bystander had tried to help the victims and sustained a fatal bullet wound when he came between the assassin and his targets.

An eyewitness had told the police and was now explaining to a television reporter how he had recently emerged from the Slug and Lettuce pub and was walking up Farringdon Street when he heard the screeching of car brakes. 'When I looked up, I 'eard a couple o' bangs like firecrackers an' I see this old fella wiv a limp – sumfin wrong wiv 'is leg anyway – sort of hoppin' as fast as 'e could towards these two young blokes up ahead, one of 'em already dahn on the pavement and the uvver cowerin' over 'im. The old fella was runnin' as fast as 'e could an' shoutin', "Git dahn, git dahn on the pavement." Then there was anuvver couple o' shots from the car – they 'ad a rifle stickin' out the car, I could see. The first bullet took dahn that plate glass winda there, and the uvver one 'it the old gent. 'E went dahn like a sack o' spuds. Bloody brave, the old fella. Then anuvver shot took care of the fella who was on 'is knees. I 'ope they get the bastards – I give the police the car reg, so they can trace that. The car went off like a bat out of 'ell.'

It was not until much later in the day that the police released the name of the innocent elderly man who had been killed: Mr James Anderton, who, the police said, was retired and had been enjoying a day's recreation in London. 'He loved going to London so much,' his wife told the press.

Chapter 16

A couple of months later, in the depths of an unusually cold winter – something to do with global warming, the pundits explained – the four bereaved wives met at the same restaurant they had used on the day their husbands died. They had forgotten that by rights Maureen should be dead also by now. It was again a lunchtime appointment, and they were met on entering (having themselves met half an hour earlier at a Café Nero) by the waiter who had been led to believe Maureen was dying from cancer. As an experienced waiter, used to disguising his real feelings about customers, he had little difficulty in dissimulating his surprise and shock at seeing Maureen so hale and hearty. And for her part, as soon as she saw the waiter, Maureen recalled her supposed terminal condition and endeavoured to look as if she was dying by putting on a mock brave-but-tortured face. She was not convincing, but how could she be? She was not ill.

Unnecessarily loudly Maureen said to Angela, believing that only she among her companions would be likely to twig what she was up to:

'Angela, dear, would you be so kind as to carry my shopping bag? It tires me so, these days, to carry anything for long'

She saw that the waiter had heard as he was meant to. Her performance worked too well, in fact. Much to her annoyance, the waiter took the liberty of offering support to Maureen by placing a hand under her elbow while directing her to a table. With his free hand he frantically gesticulated, unseen by Maureen, to a fellow waiter. The message was understood and an ordinary upright chair at the ladies' table was swiftly replaced with one out of the same stable but different, commonly referred to in furniture stores as a carver – that is, it had armrests. Maureen's waiter must have had some notion that she was at a heightened risk of falling sideways from an ordinary chair.

All seated and in possession of menus, and the waiter gone, and Maureen safe in the carver, the single ladies relaxed.

'Now I get it,' Brigitte said, almost whispering it, 'it's because 'e still sinks you are dying! I 'ad forgotten. But you look better than when we were last 'ere!'

They all laughed. They laughed so heartily that they felt ashamed. They were meeting today, in some sense at least, in commemoration of their lost husbands; laughter seemed not to be the correct way to begin. They had not all been together since the last of the cremations.

Maureen kicked off the official proceedings.

'Well, who could have believed what has actually happened to us – I mean, who would ever believe that such a sequence of events *could* happen all in the space of one day?'

'One afternoon,' Jane corrected.

Angela said: 'I'm surprised that the press and TV missed the connection between the deaths; it would have been a great story for the tabloids.'

Maureen said: 'I may have told you, but the day before their last lunch – good job it wasn't a supper! – Jim said to me he wondered whether it might be the last of their get-together lunches. He said he had a premonition.'

'Winston said something of the same sort,' Angela said; 'they all, I think, realised they were coming up to the buffers sometime soon.'

The table was quiet for a minute.

Eventually Jane said:

'One out of five men dying, when they're all are in their seventies, and all out together at lunch, is not particularly shocking, I suppose, but four of them dying and one being carried off gaga is beyond the plausible. Would be if you were a fiction writer, anyway.'

'Poor George,' Brigitte said; 'they say 'e is getting worse – no 'ope.'

'I must say,' Maureen said in her schoolteacher manner, 'that all you girls having lost your husbands at the same time has made it easier for me to bear the loss of Jim. Not, of course, that I would have wished such a fate upon any of you – you know that.'

They all agreed with Maureen. The mutuality of the day of death had made it easier for each of them to bear. They did not frame the thought in their minds, let alone contemplate verbalising it, but each of them felt that they had become members of an exclusive club that would never acquire new members and would die with them.

Maureen had thought a lot over the past two months about that day and the death of her partner and of the other husbands, and of the perhaps even worse fate of George. She now offered up one of the fruits of her cogitation:

'I'm not sure that if told they had to go, and given some choice in the matter, they wouldn't all have elected to go out in each other's company on one of their, as Jim called them, booze-ups. I suppose they did do, as near as makes no difference.'

'It wasn't quite like that, was it? Jane said.

'No, but pretty near. If they all met now and could look back on it, I think they'd see it as a hilarious ending. Not the individual deaths, for heaven's sake – no, I don't mean that – but the whole sequence; it all happening so close together, like in a French farce.'

The ladies were interrupted, but could not decide yet on food; too involved in their serious conversation, they had only glanced at the menu. They forestalled the waiter by ordering some wine and pleading for more time.

'What I think about a lot now,' Angela said, leaving time for the waiter to retreat before she spoke, 'is the years, decades actually, when Winston and I were painstakingly planning and plotting our way to make ends meet, to get our daughter educated, to put a bit aside for the old rainy day, and sometimes struggling just to keep our heads above water. Now, looking back, with Winston dead, it seems to me we wasted a lot of our life. We missed out on the living bit, if I can put it like that – when we were young. I realise now – but only now, unfortunately – how easy it is to do that. You wouldn't think it possible: you live, but you miss out on living. We did. You don't forget to eat, do you? You don't forget to sleep. But you can forget to live life, experience it – and during the best years of your life too – if all the time you're instead busy preventing it from kicking you in the teeth.

'My view today – not that any young person would be interested in it – is you've got to live, even when young and poor, not in fear of what can go wrong but rather always expecting that it will come right. Easy to say retrospectively.'

'I'm not sure I get it,' Brigitte said.

'I'm not sure I can explain it any better – perhaps because I'm not quite sure how we missed out, only that we did. It's like this: if you're always on guard against what might go wrong, you can't be open and receptive to the good things, the best things, in life – they pass you by because you're looking the other way.'

'That happens in most people's lives, I think,' Maureen said, 'at some stage. It's a question of balance.'

Angela continued:

'If any of us was asked whether we would prefer to have a life packed with experience or one that offered security but no experience, we'd all opt for experience; but it's not how we actually live, is it? How many people actually choose the safety and security of the monastery or nunnery rather than life? Not many, but lots of us nevertheless end up spending much of our lives as if seeking some version of that security and safety – always at the expense of living our lives to the full, I think.'

Maureen replied:

'You've said a mouthful, Angela. We've all got regrets about the past, for the reasons you give. We were the children of parents who'd lived through the Great Depression. They knew, our parents did, what life was like when you were poor and unemployed in the era before the Welfare State; it made them inculcate in their own children – us – an almost irrational fear of unemployment and poverty. I remember Jim telling me his dad tried his utmost to make him go into the civil service precisely because, although the pay wasn't good, the job was absolutely secure, with an absolutely secure pension. Those were the days.'

'Let's eat – but what? Jane said, looking into her menu, somewhat depressed by Angela's retrospective and Maureen's addendum.

The restaurant was beginning to get noisier – the old dears, as Maureen had suggested they ought to call themselves, though not to enthusiastic support, found their table no longer to their liking and asked to be moved to a quieter, window spot. 'Of course, of course: follow me,' their waiter said, and he carried Maureen's carver to its new location and deftly slid it under the old dear's rear as she sat down.

'This is better – quieter and a view too,' Jane said. The old dears placed their order and filled their glasses again.

Angela took up the conversation more or less where they left off.

'I think what I was saying is probably nonsense – most of what I say is!' she laughed. 'But the more I think about it the more I believe that every old person looks back and thinks they've missed out in one way or another. It's got nothing to do with your status or wealth or education. After all, we don't ever really find out what we want, or in our case, now it's all in the past: *wanted*, do we? Is it wealth, status, love, success, peace, adventure, respect? It depends – everyone wants something different, and then wants something different at different stages of their lives. And there's no evidence that wealth, or whatever – anything – brings certain happiness or satisfaction. A modicum of discontent – at least a modicum – is necessary to keep us motivated: it's nature's plan. Must be.'

'Stress and difficulty certainly brings out the best in some people,' Maureen said. 'Churchill was asked towards the end of his life which year he'd choose to live over again: his answer, which he had no doubt about, was nineteen forty, the Battle of Britain year, when we fought alone. So for him, the year of greatest stress, anxiety, doubt and fear was his highlight; he'd have liked to go through it all over again in preference to all the years of adulation and security that followed the war. What do you make of that?'

'What do *you* make of it?' Jane asked.

'Perhaps we really enjoyed those difficult years when we were struggling to make ends meet,' Maureen teased. 'Which year of *our* lives would *we* choose as the one we'd most enjoy living over again, I wonder?'

'Sounds like a new game show,' Jane said.

'Is a good question, I sink,' Brigitte said.

Food arrived just as all of the old dears keenly wanted to talk about the best years of their lives.

'For me and Ben the best years were those when the girls were still all under ten years old. I know 'e would 'ave agreed wis me,' Brigitte said. She had a tear in her eye.

The same thought occurred to them all, and Jane gave it voice:

'Brigitte is right. The best years were the early years. Wouldn't we all agree that?'

Maureen said:

'You're right, of course, Brigitte; and by the way, I don't believe people who say their lives were perfectly happy and they have no regrets. I have regrets; Jim had regrets; I'm sure you all and your husbands had some regrets and disappointments. That's life. What makes the struggle and disappointments, the regrets too, all bearable and life worth the candle is – I hope this doesn't sound straight out of *Woman's Own* – is if there is love in your life. And this needn't be marital, or for children or family – I mean love in its widest sense. If you have work you love, a hobby you love, art, sport – any attachment that's strong enough to make you willing to put up with the trials and tribulations...'

Angela had an example and could not resist interrupting: 'Stephen Hawkins, for example. Would he have gone on so long if he hadn't had his love of physics?'

'Exactly,' Maureen said, forgiving Angela's interruption immediately since it supplied the clincher to her argument. 'Exactly.'

Jane looked agitated; she had been pushing food around on her plate for a minute, trying to decide whether and how to raise another subject.

Brigitte looked at her wonderingly. 'What's wrong, Jane? Food's okay, isn't it?'

'Well...it's just that...well, we're here today because our husbands are all dead. Shouldn't we talk about them, or something?'

'I thought we were, in a roundabout sort of way,' Angela said, a bit affronted at the hint of callousness.

'Jane's right,' Maureen said, 'we should give them a toast. Let's order a bottle of champagne and raise a glass to thank them and wish them bon voyage.'

They all felt it was the thing to do – it justified the lunch, gave it meaning. When the glasses were filled, Maureen poured; they raised their glasses, all now looking in Maureen's direction for no other reason than because she had filled the glasses, and resoundingly shouted: 'Thanks and bon voyage!'

There were tears in everyone's eyes, including their waiter's. Standing leaning against the cutlery and crockery cabinet with a colleague beside him, the waiter had heard the toast and seen Angela, Jane and Brigitte raise their glasses to Maureen, and, as it appeared to him from a distance, wish *her* bon voyage.

'That's one gutsy old lady,' the waiter said to his companion, deeply moved, as his companion could see from the tears trickling down his cheeks.

'Why – what do you mean?' the companion asked, himself not having observed the toast.

'That frail old lady in the armchair has a terminal cancer – she can't have long to go because she told me about it last time they were here a couple of months ago. I suppose the end is imminent. What you didn't see, Henry, is that just now, with that champagne there, they all toasted her and wished her bon voyage. Wished her bon voyage, bloody hell! Talk about stiff upper lip – she's as game as they come. I hope my old mum goes out like that. It's a privilege to serve her.'

Angela, addressing no one in particular, instead looking beyond their cluttered table and through the window, where the day itself was now dying a cold damp bleak death that none would mourn, said:

'And now our lifelong partners are gone, do we still have love enough invested in this world? To make the struggle worth continuing, I mean? Who or what needs or wants our love now? Is my love of playing Chopin ballades (very badly, of course) – is that going to keep me invested in the game?'

'It's easy to get depressed at our age; it was easy even before our husbands died – speaking for myself anyway,' Jane said.

'Look,' Maureen said, 'we'll plod on – that's what people do. Didn't Andy have a saying – keep buggering on, KBO – well, that's what we're going to do. And it needn't be too awful. I have a suggestion. It's this: our old men met at the pub every couple of months, religiously – let's take up the baton and start by meeting at the Nell Gwynne in a month or two, in their honour and for our own continuing sanity. You never know, perhaps people will begin to talk about us, look down their noses disapprovingly. Old age is the time for notoriety. What have we to lose? We might become a legend. When they think of us and our get-togethers for pub or restaurant lunches, it will be as – what!? The Old Women and the Pub! What about that?'

The old ladies roared with laughter.

Their special waiter looked on admiringly, shaking his head in disbelief. Brigitte began suddenly to cry. A sudden wind rattled the windowpanes of the restaurant, and it began to rain heavily. The noise of the wind and rain gusting against the windows distracted customers and interrupted conversation.

End